SWEETER THAN WINE

L. NEIL SMITH AT PHOENIX PICK

SWEETER THAN WINE

L. NEIL SMITH

an imprint of

MANOR

Rockville, Maryland

Tarikian, TARK Classic Fiction, Arc Manor, Arc Manor Classic Reprints, Phoenix Pick, Phoenix Rider, Manor Thrift and logos associated with those imprints are trademarks or registered trademarks of Arc Manor Publishers, Rockville, Maryland. All other trademarks and trademarked names are properties of their respective owners.

This book is presented as is, without any warranties (implied or otherwise) as to the accuracy of the production, text or translation.

ISBN: 978-1-60450-483-5

www.PhoenixPick.com
Great Science Fiction at Great Prices

Visit the Author's Website at:
http://www.lneilsmith.org

Visit the Author's Page at Phoenix Pick:
http://www.ElNeil.com

Published by Phoenix Pick
an imprint of Arc Manor
P. O. Box 10339
Rockville, MD 20849-0339
www.ArcManor.com

To Rylla and Jen, who got me into this.

♈

ACKNOWLEDGEMENT

Most of *Sweeter Than Wine* was written in November, 2009 as my participation in the zany and wonderful National Novel Writing Month, otherwise known as NaNoWriMo. Each year, thousands of people, mostly young, who have a story to tell and would otherwise never have gotten it told, promise each other to write 50,000 words in 30 silly and exhausting days. I've wanted to tell this story for nearly thirty years and now, thanks to NaNoWriMo, here it is.

Check out http://www.nanowrimo.org/

I'd also like to thank my friends Curt Howland and Ken Valentine for making this a better book than it would have been without their help.

Very special thanks to Cathy.

♈

Sufficient unto the day is the evil thereof.

—*Matthew 6:34*

CONTENTS

THE TRAVELER: CHARLESTON

"Time sweeps everything before it, and can bring with it good as well as evil, and evil as well as good."—Niccolo Machiavelli

The electronic alarm, set for the date as well as the time, went off. It took a long while to shake off weeks of unconsciousness that had come before it, one hour, two hours, three...the traveler never looked.

Outside, it was nighttime, exactly as planned. At the traveler's order, before the long sea voyage, a small hole had been bored in the face of the otherwise anonymous freighter container. A kind of lens—nothing more than a two-centimeter-thick rod of clear glass three millimeters in diameter, set in a finely threaded metal collar—had been screwed into it, absolutely inconspicuous, even to a careful observer. From the outside of the container, it would merely look like a mechanical excrescence, a bolt or something else that no one would ever pay any attention to. From inside the container, it would offer the traveler life and death evidence about what time of day it really was.

Clocks, after all, can go wrong.

The traveler unfastened the cot's retaining straps—the cot itself was bolted to the floor—stood up, laid hands on a medium-sized canvas shoulder bag, already neatly packed, and unlaced it from the lashing holes that had held it in place on one wall no matter how the container might be tossed about. Everything else—the cot, the sanitary facility hardly used, a small, battery-powered cooler whose precious contents the traveler now exhausted—was meant to be left behind.

Toward the front end of the container, as quietly as possible, the traveler bent the splayed ends of a lightweight cotter pin where they passed through a thumb-thick steel shaft, extracted the pin, turned the shaft, which served as a handle lever, and heard with satisfaction the locking mechanism on the outside of the container make a thunking noise.

Cautiously the right-hand door was swung open, admitting fresh, damp, cool air, laden with the odors of salt water, dead fish, rotted sea vegetation, and several varieties of lubricant and marine motor fuel. There were noises to go with it: splashing at the fringes of the harbor, distant bells, the horn of a tugboat laboring through the darkness.

The traveler stepped out onto the concrete surface of the dock, dazzled momentarily by the starlight, a sliver of cloud-wisped moon, the city lights of a hundred different colors across the water that reflected them. These were the lights, thought the traveler—who had never ventured to North America before—of Charleston, South Carolina.

From the canvas bag, the traveler produced a fist-sized egg-shaped plastic object, another item made especially to order by a very highly skilled—and normally quite lavishly compensated—artisan, now deceased.

The traveler, who had employed this extraordinary individual, and his father and grandfather before him, on many previous occasions, was leaving Europe for the foreseeable future, and had no further use for the man. Because Interpol was all too well aware of his existence and his activities on behalf of the traveler and others, the unfortunate fellow represented a potentially dangerous loose end that must be discarded.

The traveler removed another cotter pin, this one on a pull-ring, from the top of the device, being careful to throw them back into the container. A lever, curving from top to bottom of the device, and made from a stamped piece of sheet steel a centimeter wide, was released to fly after them. The traveler tossed the device inside the container, onto the cot, shut and locked the door from the outside, and was two hundred meters away before it went off, soundlessly, without visible flame.

There would be no explosion. There would be no fire. Everything in the container, including the paint on its walls, ceiling, and floor, the cot and bedding, tiny cooler, contents of the portable lavatory, and every single fingerprint, would quietly smolder into a fine white ash.

The colorful city lights twinkled across the water, beckoning to the traveler, making promises about movement, warmth, life, and easy prey.

A few minutes later, more or less as the traveler had anticipated, a middle-aged, slightly overweight individual wearing an ill-fitting uniform, reeking with human perspiration, approached from near the junction of the dock and the shoreline proper, where seemingly endless rows of big metal warehouses disappeared into the distance, right and left.

There were probably security cameras hanging everywhere—it was getting to be like that as the ridiculous human species grew more and more afraid of itself, when there were better (or far worse) things to be afraid of in this world—but at the moment, that couldn't be helped.

"Excuse me, U.S. Customs. This is a restricted impounding and quarantine area," the man said, shining a long, obscenely brilliant flashlight into the traveler's face. "You need to show me some I.D., please."

The traveler, who had first learned the English language fifteen centuries earlier, being forced to relearn it several times as it had evolved into what the man was speaking now, nodded, swiftly stepping closer to the guard, seizing him one-handedly by the throat, dragging him into the black shadows of a small building on the dock. The guard tried making noises, then groped desperately for the revolver at his belt.

Whimsically, the traveler let him do it, almost enjoying the icy hot sensation as the trigger was pulled over and over again, thrusting six rapidly-expanding lead-cored, cupronickel-jacketed projectiles into the traveler's abdomen. As the half dozen hollowpoints blossomed within the traveler like lethal flowers, the bodies of the traveler and the guard muffled the noise. When it was over, the traveler pulled the guard closer, exposing outsized upper canine incisors the victim was allowed to see before they sank into his neck at the carotid artery.

He died making gurgling noises as the traveler drank him dry. The bullet wounds had already closed and begun healing from the inside. The bullets would migrate out of the wounds within the next couple of days.

The scars would vanish in a week.

The traveler left the body in a nearby dumpster, jumped a 12-foot chainlink fence topped with a coil of razor wire, and headed for the city.

Where lights were bright and there were a hundred thousand other throats. Waiting.

1: BORN EVERY MINUTE

"No man chooses evil because it is evil; he only mistakes it for happiness."—Mary Wollstonecraft

My client was writing me a check as fast as he could.

It was a big check, I don't work cheap.

He was in a hurry because he was an idiot. I had just proven to his satisfaction that Charlene, his curvaceous blond secretary, was the baddie who'd been embezzling from his office for the past six months. She was an idiot, too; she'd come with him to this meeting, probably thinking her long eyelashes, sexy hips, and magnificent mammaries would protect her from anything. Now she was being taken away by two very young, uniformed representatives of the New Prospect Police Department.

That's New Prospect, Colorado, a little old-fashioned town of shady, tree-lined brick-paved avenues, snuggled at the feet of the Rockies, altogether too near the northern edge of the capital city, Denver.

Dum, da dum dum.

I liked the printed jersey dress that clung to Charlene's body like a wisp of smoke. It reminded me of the way girls looked in movies I'd gone to see as a kid, back in rural east-central Illinois. There was even a chance that the tears presently spoiling her eye makeup were real. Allowing for her 21st century hairstyle, she resembled Jean Harlow a little, which was a shame, because she wasn't going to look nearly as good in the orange jumpsuit Hamilton County would be issuing her.

My client finished with me and jumped up. "Don't worry, Charlene!" he hollered at her back as they marched her through my front door. "I'll come down and pay your bail! You'll see, everything will be all right!"

No it wouldn't be, but it wasn't my job to tell him. It was my job to straighten things out afterward, in case she killed him, or he killed her, or his wife killed them both. Even then, I don't normally do murders if I can avoid them. For an unlicensed private investigator (I like to think of myself as an "equalizer") working from his home, discreetly offering his services, there just isn't any money in them. Only dead people and people who, one way or another, wind up dead inside.

It was getting late. When cops and client and culprit were gone—I watched the patrol car pull away from the curb, the client's BMW taillights right behind it—I dead bolted the front door, turned out the porch light, put the check and the Xeroxes of Charlene's questionable ledger entries away in the safe (copies would go to the District Attorney and the client's lawyer in the morning), turned the office lights out, and headed for the kitchen at the back of the house.

I would have set the house alarm—I've made plenty of folks hate me over the years—but I don't have one. I can hear a pin drop 200 yards away. To me, owing to the peculiar capabilities and limitations of my situation, it sounds just like a manhole cover falling off a truck. Besides, as late as it was, I wouldn't be going to bed until morning.

I heard a quiet "Meow?" and glanced toward the hall to the first floor bedroom. Fiddlestring had come out of hiding. The big orange tiger-stripe hates company. When we have visitors, he lurks under the bed and plots, like a James Bond villain, to have them all killed. He attacked a little girl once—a weird, scary little girl with an even weirder, scarier mommy—who had herded him into a corner where he couldn't back up any more. She should have known better, he'd given her plenty of warning, hissing and spitting and growling as cats will. When she lunged for him, he went around one bare leg like an oldtime patented apple peeling machine, and she not only howled, she wet her panties.

Her mother, a client determined to get the goods on hubby, was outraged that I didn't pull my .38 out then and there and blow that animal's head off, or something equally emphatic. I said her little girl had simply gotten what she'd deserved. Damned if she didn't hire me anyway, and paid me promptly (they always do). Turned out that her husband was only hiding out in the New Prospect Public Library to get away, if only for an hour or two, from the weird, scary females in his life.

I didn't blame him a bit.

Fiddlestring sawed back and forth, threatening to trip me.

I reached down and scratched his head roughly, working on the ears. Truth is, male cats basically think they're dogs. They like to be roughed up, shoulder-punched, shadow-boxed, and wrestled with like a bunch of Broncos fans watching the Superbowl together. You could hear him purr all the way across the room, like somebody mowing the damn lawn outside your bedroom window. "How'd you like something to eat?"

"Meow!"

In the kitchen, I opened and decanted a can of smoked oysters for Fiddlestring, fixed myself a cup of strong coffee, and made a peanut butter and chutney sandwich. That would take care of my stomach, but a familiar sensation told me that before tomorrow morning, I'd have to *feed*.

A vampire doesn't live on peanut butter alone.

2: DANCING IN THE DARK

"When choosing between two evils, I always like to try
the one I've never tried before."—*Mae West*

To begin with, it's a virus.

A symbiotic virus: I treat it right and it protects me from disease, aging, and injury. Physically, it makes me extremely strong.

I can't fly, or turn into a bat, but after an unfortunate accident I had with a bandsaw back in the 50s, I discovered that I can grow a pinky back—and that severed body parts turn to fine, gray ash. My finger, lying there on the saw table, quickly came to resemble a burnt cigar.

The virus also has certain legendary weaknesses. It can't stand the direct sun because ultraviolet light destroys it, quite violently. (Don't ask me how I learned that; you don't want to know.) Garlic will kill it, too. I've watched that drama play out a hundred times through the microscope. Even related vegetables like onions and leeks make me queasy.

Likewise, direct contact with metallic silver has much the same nasty, cauterizing effect on my virus-permeated flesh that contact with silver nitrate has on ordinary, uninfected human beings. Think about table salt on a garden slug. Whenever I handle silver objects—reasonably often in my particular line of work—I have to wear gloves.

On the other hand, I *can* see my own image perfectly well in a mirror. How many laws of physics would you have to repeal for it to be any other way? And as for a stake through the heart, who *wouldn't* die?

Me, that's who.

Ironically, the vampire virus would seal the wound up—instantly fatal to any ordinary individual—until it healed. But even vampires appear to have had their superstitions. Research tells me it was only a piece of the True Cross that was supposed to have been lethal to them.

I wonder whether you could find something like that on eBay.

Sorry to de-romanticize it, but there you are. It is, as they say, what it is. It's a very old, very primitive, very large virus that you can actually see for yourself if you have a fairly good optical microscope.

I got my dose a couple of weeks after D-Day. Having unexpectedly survived the terrors of Omaha Beach, I got separated from my unit (I was a Second Lieutenant and I guess nobody missed me) and wound up alone in a picturesque little French village about twenty minutes before it got overrun by the badguys trying to arrange a resurgence against the invasion.

In a little postcard-perfect but abandoned house, it didn't take long to discover a cleverly concealed wine cellar—the French had made a fine art of hiding their best stuff from the soldiers of all nations—behind a false wall in a basement. Outside, it was bright and sunny, houses surprisingly pristine in their whitewashed glory. I pulled the fake wall into place behind me and sat in the dank, stuffy, musty-smelling darkness for an hour, trying to figure out what to do next.

Before I really noticed it, I wasn't smelling mildew any more, but something else, something elusive, evocative, giving me a feeling that was all wrong, considering where I was and what was going on. Outside, I could hear the Huns in combat boots stomping up and down the little street. I could hear the occasional car, and even an armored personnel carrier. Once or twice, aircraft that didn't sound like our own flew overhead.

And still the sensation that was half aroma and half imaginary spiders crawling up and down my spine persisted. I squatted where I was, one hand on my sidearm in its flapped issue holster, thinking how good a drink of wine would be right now, if only I could make myself move.

Move!

I whirled, and reached behind me in the darkness, my outstretched hand landing on something I hadn't felt since Sally Danforth had given me a spectacular send-off in her father's hayloft the day after I'd graduated from the local aggie college and enlisted in the United States Army. That Hitler was going to get his, now that I was in the fight!

My hand, it seemed, had found a breast. A very warm, very soft, moderately large breast. A left breast, to be precise, under what felt to me like a uniform shirt. For some reason I didn't withdraw my hand immediately (normally, I'm somewhat bashful, and that would have been my reflexive response at any other time, on any other day, in any other war), but kept it where it was, instead, enjoying what it was feeling.

A soft voice said, "Do you like that one? I have another, very similar."

The voice, of course, was feminine, low and a little breathy, with just the faintest brush of tongue and teeth on the esses, not quite a lisp, which for some reason I'd always found very attractive. It was also accented: eastern European of some sort, but not Polish. I'd met quite a few of them, attached to my battalion: exiles helping us to free their country from the murderous fascist horror that had engulfed it.

But she wasn't Polish, she was something else. Right now, I didn't really care what. Still holding onto her in that odd manner, I was thinking that, whatever happened now—even if she just shot me—a little wine would go great with it. Then I realized what that aroma had been: girl-breath garnished with just a trace of alcoholic grape juice.

Sally and I had been getting into her father's winter-aged hard cider that night in rural Illinois. Nowadays I guess behavioral scientists would call that an imprinting experience. For some reason, still sitting there on the cellar floor, I let go of her breast (temporarily, I rushed to assure myself), reached around the back of her neck—I still remember the sensation of feeling the soft, silky short hair back there where the rest had been combed up into a French braid or something—pulled her invisible face to mine and kissed her.

It was just like somebody had pushed a dynamite plunger. Clothing exploded from our bodies in every direction and I was on her, riveting our bodies together with no thought for the implacable foe outside, the dirty cellar floor beneath us, or much of anything else. I'd never felt that way before and I haven't since, but it happened every single time we came together. She was long-legged and lithe and at the same time seemed to be composed entirely of curves. She was smooth, but very firm beneath that feminine softness, and she just plain smelled *right*.

Like the pie table at a county fair.

Then there was another explosion, and I saw the white light that the mystics blather about. As we lay there together afterward, both of us wishing we had cigarettes, she said, in her low, breathy, aromatic, and unidentifiably accented voice, "Now we will take our time, lovely man. We certainly have no lack of it. The Germans aren't going away soon."

Lovely man. Nobody had ever called me that. Nobody has since then. "My name is J. Gifford. The J doesn't stand for anything, see, because—" Actually, I had told her my real name which I haven't used in years.

She placed a finger on my lips. "I am Surica. *Your* Surica, at the moment."

And she was.

THE TRAVELER: ATLANTA, GEORGIA

"No evil dooms us hopelessly except the evil we love, and desire to continue in, and make no effort to escape from."—*George Eliot*

The witching hour.

The traveler shook hands with the driver, exchanged a few parting pleasantries with her, shouldered the canvas bag, and climbed from a tractor that might otherwise have been exited easily with a casual hop.

Appearances were important at the moment. True nature could come later.

Likewise, it would have been convenient and pleasant to feed right here and now, in the privacy of a vehicle that was almost a rolling apartment in and of itself. But cross-continental operators like this one perceived themselves as part of a culture set aside from the rest of the nation-state, and they were astonishingly protective of one another.

This much the traveler had learned from the driver, apparently a rather lonely woman, recently widowed, who had required only a modicum of persuasive pressure before offering transportation—illegally, as it developed, or against her company's regulations (it had never been entirely clear)—from a place in Charleston almost exactly like this one, a "giant food and fuel plaza," to this specimen, located at the western edge of Atlanta, Georgia. Free shower with every fill-up, long distance telephones, and multidenominational church services every Sunday. A woman, the traveler had reasoned, would be safer to travel with.

Along the way she had regaled the traveler with stories of a life on the road with her husband, with whom she had had many adventures—at least she considered them so—until he had succumbed suddenly to a heart attack in the fairly recent past, nearly taking her and a load of self-sealing stem bolts with him. The traveler told her stories, too, of a long life in Europe, Asia, and Africa, not all of them made up.

Now, walking all the way around the enormous main building—fuel desk, restaurant, half a dozen shops of various kinds—to the back, the traveler waited patiently in a deeply shadowed corner of a huge area otherwise lit as brightly as daytime. Patience was rewarded in a little while when a young woman wearing the uniform of a waitress came through a back door with a large full plastic trash bag in her hands, headed for one of the dumpsters that ubiquitously dotted the American landscape.

In a moment, the traveler had her and, unwilling to feed in the unaesthetic pen around the garbage disposal facilities, laid a hand over her mouth and, ignoring her desperate flailing, zigzagged from the shadow of one semi-tractor to the shadow of another, carrying her to a grassy field at the edge of the asphalt where a drainage ditch had been visible as the truck from Charleston had pulled into the big lot.

The ditch grew deeper into the soil until it ended at the mouth of a culvert, a concrete tube at least four feet in diameter, running all the way under the interstate. It was obstructed by heavy screening—wire the diameter of pencils arranged in eight centimeter squares—at both ends, almost certainly to prevent indigents from sleeping in it.

Effortlessly, the traveler took the girl into the culvert, never said a word to her, but without prelude tore the side of her throat open, and as the highway traffic passed over their heads at 100 kilometers an hour, bathed them both in what escaped the predator's maw. It was possible, the traveler knew from centuries of experience, to feed lightly this way, making up the deficit with human food, but why bother when the fare at hand was alive and hot and sweeter than wine?

For many a lifetime, the traveler had carefully chosen clothing that could be bled on and only show it minimally. This was necessary when there was much traveling to be done or business with the humans who were stupid, for the most part, but amazingly inventive and productive. Later there were fabrics available that could be easily cleaned. The traveler almost loved humans for making everything so easy.

Abandoning the dead and emptied waitress, the traveler was inside the truckstop swiftly, purchased a ticket for a shower from another tasty-looking young woman behind a counter who would retain no memory of the transaction (perhaps she would do for breakfast if they were still here), found the shower room, hung up the bag, and stepped into the enclosure fully clothed, allowing the evidence to swirl down the drain.

According to the guidebook, Atlanta has a humid, subtropical climate, so it was necessary to dry everything electrically, passing a dangerous and vulnerable hour wearing only a towel. Fortunately, it was a slow night at the truck stop, and even slower at this end of the building. The time was spent listening to "Your Cheatin' Heart," "Hey, Good Lookin'," and other, similar selections on the overhead music system.

Drinking reasonably decent coffee in the truck stop restaurant—in here, the musical selections appeared to range from "Jambalaya" to "Cold, Cold Heart" (the traveler examined the jukebox carefully, wondering exactly who this Hank Williams was and why he was obsessed with hearts; had he had vampire tendencies, himself?)—it was fairly easy to find another ride headed further west. Clearly, North America was not at all like tiny, cozy Europe. There was still a long way to go.

This time the driver was a middle-aged male, unshaven, unshowered, and reeking of cigar smoke. The man, the traveler thought, seemed to have a bit of a mean streak not very well hidden underneath. He had to be offered money and gaped like an illiterate peasant at the pair of gold coins the traveler proffered. Perhaps the trucking brotherhood would not protect this one so assiduously. Perhaps the thing to do was order something now—what in the name of all eternity was a chicken fried steak?—and do the important feeding at the other end of the line.

And get the gold coins back.

And perhaps find a source of some decent music. The traveler had always enjoyed Mozart until the fellow had given up too much blood and died.

3: ACCIDENTAL TRUTH

"Evil is always possible. And goodness is
eternally difficult."—*Anne Rice*

Captain Anton Varick and I go back quite a way. He'd been a fuzzy-cheeked rookie beat cop in beautiful downtown New Prospect when he and I first met. I'd just moved into town, trying to figure out what to do with myself. Now he was Chief of Detectives for the small force, and I am...

Well, whatever I am.

It was the next morning. I'd come downtown, as promised, to sign off on some paperwork for the patrol guys who'd taken Charlene off my hands. While I was there, I'd decided to visit my old friend Anton. The building was old, brick and stone, probably built by the W.P.A. in the 1930s, like a lot of civic architecture across this part of the country.

Anton's office had a hardwood floor, high ceiling, and windows to go with it. There was an air conditioner stuck into one of them, but I'd never seen it operating. The old building was just naturally cool. In winter, a pair of big cast iron radiators with so many layers of paint you could no longer make out the decorative details made hissing noises.

"Come on in, Giff," he told me when he saw me standing at his open office door. He was the only one who called me that. Good guy that I am, I let him. "And close the door behind you. Had your morning coffee yet?"

As a matter of fact, I had, courtesy of Starbucks, but I didn't say so. Instead I let him pour me a paper cup from the carafe of his Mr. Coffee—I take mine black—and sat down across from him at his desk. I took a sip. It was the only decent coffee I'd ever had inside a police station. The virus just loves caffeine, and I could almost hear the little guys going "Whoopee!" and doing cartwheels in my blood vessels.

"How's it going, Anton?" I was the only one who called him that. To all others, including his wife, Priscilla, a nice lady and a great cook—except for those who called him "sir"—he was Varick or just "Vare."

"Not too well, I'm afraid." He was tall and lean, what they call "rangy," and no suit off the rack was ever going to fit him right. His big face was long and sort of pleated, flesh punctuated by vertical ridges and gullies. At the moment, Anton looked terrible, as if he'd been up all night, crying. He said, "Pris had a routine exam a couple of weeks ago. I insisted on it. They found something, Giff, something really bad. She's in the hospital overnight tonight, doing more tests. But it's cancer, ovarian cancer. They say she doesn't have much time left."

I knew she'd been sick. I had no idea she'd been that sick. The bad news chilled me right through to the bottom of whatever I use for a soul. These people were the closest thing I'd had to a family since France.

In a way, Anton was the reason that I do what I do. When I first arrived in New Prospect, looking to put down roots after wandering for years, Ronald Reagan was the President, William Powell—the "Thin Man"—had just passed away, and I was between cars. It was a cloudy, overcast day in late March. Mostly, I'm active at night, but I can go out in daylight, especially if it's cloudy, with protective clothing, sunblock, and my big, floppy hat—one reason I'd moved west to the Denver area is that nobody looks at you funny if you wear a big floppy hat.

Indoors, or at night, I prefer well-worn jeans, cowboy boots, and aloha shirts depicting sunny tropics I will never see for myself. Sometimes I think I should move to Seattle where it's cloudy all the time.

I'd been sitting on a bench at a bus stop, thinking about cars and houses. An old man sat at the other end of the bench, sort of twisted away from me, muttering something into the fraying lapels of his dirty topcoat.

Almost without thinking, I asked, "What did you say?"

The old man turned, compelled by my question. I have that effect on people. It isn't hypnosis. I don't know what the hell it is. I just ask folks, straightforwardly and in a perfectly normal voice, to do things, or to tell me things, and they always seem happy to comply. Admittedly, it's a pretty handy skill for an investigator, but I have to be extremely careful never to use it when I consider it unethical to.

Like on a date.

At any rate, the old man proceeded to tell me, in the most loving, gut-curdling detail, about a pretty young woman he'd murdered with a flensing knife in Wales in 1917. And then another one he'd killed in 1918. And then in 1919. And then 1920, the year I'd been born. His story took a long, long time to tell. He was a monster who remembered each and every organ he'd cut from his helpless victims' still-living flesh.

He was sickeningly eloquent about the way it had smelled.

Making it sound more like a résumé than a confession, once the stopper had been pulled on secrets he'd been keeping inside for almost 70 years, there wasn't any way to shut him up. Eventually relocating to Canada, and then on to America after the First World War, he'd managed, or so he informed me, to mutilate and butcher at least one attractive female victim every year until the late 1960s, when one of his potential targets had shot him in the groin, and he'd only barely managed to get away. Now, at 90, he was too old and crippled to have any more fun—that's just how he described it—and he was deeply bitter.

If it was true, at least four dozen mangled corpses in at least three countries made this old son of a bitch a world-class serial killer. I'd have gladly finished him off myself, on the spot, or made him commit suicide (I'd never done anything like that before, but I was pretty sure I could), but it would have been too easy. He was in a lot of pain from arthritis and other stuff. I wanted him to stay that way, maybe with a heaping helping of humiliation and defeat for good measure. I considered asking him to feel more pain, but restrained myself.

Of course it could all turn out to be utter bullshit. On my way to the bus stop from the real estate office where I'd been exploring housing possibilities that morning, I'd noticed a young policeman on foot patrol, one I'd seen before over the past several days exploring beautiful downtown New Prospect, and now had a nodding acquaintance with.

Glancing around, I saw him again, across the street. Turning to the old man, I said, "Stay put!" I crossed the street, a grassy median where there were still iron trolley tracks, and then the other half of the street. The cop noticed me coming toward him and raised his eyebrows.

"Officer," I said, once I was within earshot, my voice growing quieter as I got closer. "That old man over at the bus stop is saying some amazing things. I think you'd better come over and listen to him."

The nametag on the cop's pocket flap said "Varick, A."

4: UNETHICAL ALTRUISM

"I have a strong moral sense—by my standards."—Rex Stout

*T*here wasn't really anything to say, but you try, anyway.

"I'm sorry, Anton." I'd known Priscilla Varick for twenty-five years. She was from some tiny town in Indiana, so I identified with her. She'd come here to Colorado to attend the state university in Boulder.

Anton had been writing her a parking ticket and she had decided to argue with him. That's how it starts, sometimes. First time I'd seen her she'd been eight months pregnant with their first kid and cute as a kitten, herself. In her mid-forties now, Priscilla was still more than merely an attractive woman. "Is there anything at all that I can do?"

My big hat and long coat lay across the other hardbacked office chair. His office was furnished with great big oak filing cabinets with brass fixtures, scrounged from the county school system when they switched to the ever-so-much-more-aesthetically-appealing gray sheet metal. Add a clutch of oak chairs, including the old swivel thing he sat in, and a big refinished oak table instead of a desk, where he could spread photos and other evidence. The place smelled like First Grade.

A neat little Sony laptop sat on the table. The desktop image showed the family in the right field seats at Coors Field, home of the Colorado Rockies: Anton, Priscilla, their son Patrick, currently a sophomore at the Air Force Academy and sister Amber, away at college in Vermont. Turns out that time flies whether you're having fun or not.

I'd also taken off the gloves I wear to protect the vulnerable backs of my hands. Anton's family believed I had lupus, or porphyria, or something like that. Over the years, I had deliberately left it vague.

Anton shrugged. "Not a thing, Giff. Not a thing anybody can do. Not a single. God. Damned. Thing." He sat quietly for a minute, fists closed tight atop his chair arms. "The absolute hell of it is, in spite of myself, some part of me has already started imagining life without her, although what that part can't imagine is why I'd want to live it."

My old friend reeked of fear, of anger, and of resignation.

I nodded, indicating sympathy more than understanding. I'd never really loved anybody that way, myself, although given more of a chance—more than a few weeks, for example, in some Frenchman's hidden wine cellar—I very likely could have. In my life, it was a lot less like being in love and a lot more like being haunted. That's just one of many reasons those dates I theorized about are kind of few and far between.

But Anton had it wrong. There was something I could do about Priscilla, something that nobody else I knew about could do. If necessary, I could drag Anton's wife back from the very brink of death. But there was more than a chance that I couldn't heal her without bringing her over. So the question was, would either of them thank me afterward? I liked living my life. Would they like living my life?

I'd have to think it over.

He changed the subject. "Your wayward secretary made bail this morning."

"Charlene? Not my secretary. The very thought gives me the cold shivers." There are worse things in the world than vampires and she was several of them. "Someone else's. I knew she would. He bailed her out. He said he would." I leaned back in my chair and took a sip of coffee.

Anton chuckled and shook his head. In his job he saw a lot of human folly. I did, too, in mine. What we were really feeling was gratitude that we weren't under the thrall of that particular siren. We could have been. Live long enough, or read enough history, and you'll discover that human folly—and the little head's capacity for it—is infinite. "Yeah, well, he called an hour ago to tell us she's jumped. He wants us to put out 'APBs and stuff,' but please don't hurt her."

"I figured that one, too," I laughed out loud. "The girl has no redeeming qualities whatever—well, maybe a couple of redeeming qualities."

He got up and waggled the coffee carafe at me. I nodded, and he poured more for both of us. It was good and it was helping him to talk.

"Yeah, I watched her being booked last night and couldn't help noticing those redeeming qualities, both of them." He changed the subject again. "Look, I'm going out to the range after dark. Want to come?"

"Sure." Dark was the only time I could really practice outdoors. And here was something else I could do for my old friend. Like a lot of cops, Anton tends to keep things bottled up. He can let them go amidst loud noises, brilliant muzzle flashes, harsh recoil, and the sweet scent of burned nitrocellulose. I'm like that, too. "Your car or mine?"

We made our arrangements. My car: an elderly Suburban with a huge rebuilt engine and transmission and heavily smoked windows. I could pass the day in that thing if I had to, it was almost a rolling motel room. I also had an off-white Plymouth PT Cruiser I'd accepted in lieu of payment from an otherwise worthy client who was down on his luck. I'd straightened that out for him easily, but it would take him a long while to recover. I hadn't been able to resist the car. It had a sun roof.

I got out of the chair, glanced backward to make sure the door was well shut, looked at Anton and said, "Pocomoco." Without a word or hesitation, Anton loosened his necktie. We'd been through this ritual about once a week for the past quarter of a century or so. My friend wasn't really in some kind of trance, he just looked that way. Like I said, I don't believe it's hypnosis, but I really don't know what it is.

Getting the kit from my coat, I swabbed his neck with an alcohol wipe and sank the needle of a disposable Vacutainer into the artery. It filled quickly. I tucked it away for later. I didn't need much. The blood feeds the virus, not the vampire. A second needle, hair fine, went into the vein inside my left elbow and withdrew fifty microliters of my own blood, which I injected directly into friend Anton's pulsing jugular.

Over the years, I've worked out an ethic that guides this part of my life. As long as I don't drain a victim (I've never come anywhere near it), my "bite," the transfer of a little of my blood, is a good thing, temporarily conveying some of the same attributes to the person "bitten" that I, myself enjoy permanently, without turning them into vampires. I never take advantage of a client, or someone with whom I'm currently intimate. As I said, the latter doesn't seem to happen very often.

So no, I wasn't turning Anton into a vampire. Despite the nonsense you see on TV, it takes a lot more effort than that, several weeks of a more or less constant exchange of bodily fluids. Let him get his own girl for that. But everybody always says that Anton heals remarkably quickly. He is aging with both style and grace, and hasn't had a cold or flu—or anything else—for...well, for about a quarter of a century.

I haven't actually bitten anyone for years.

Too messy.

THE TRAVELER: MEMPHIS, TENNESSEE

"I have put before you today, life and good,
and death and evil."—The Torah

*S*ometimes even monsters encounter monsters.

The traveler knew well that there were worse things in the world than vampires. Most of them were humans—or had presumably started out that way—that had to be disposed of on one's journey through life, lest the hue and cry arising on their account threaten one's own existence.

Jack the Ripper had been one of those.

There were vampires, ranging from the merely indiscreet to the suicidally flamboyant, that had to be disposed of, too, for similar reasons.

It was annoying, especially in that it served to benefit humanity, natural prey for whom the traveler felt a certain understandable...well the proper expression was not contempt, exactly. The traveler tried to think of it as an act of animal husbandry—the way a shepherd might kill a wolf to keep it out of the fold—but it still rankled.

Not that the occasional Erzsebet Bathory, Jack the Ripper, H.H. Holmes, Albert Fish, Ted Bundy—no, not even Lenin, Hitler, Stalin, Mao, or Pol Pot—endangered the human species in any way. There were almost seven billion of the organisms in the world now. The expression "breed like rabbits" should be amended to "breed like Homo sapiens", instead.

The driver who had been persuaded to offer the traveler a ride outside of Atlanta had turned out to be one such human monster, revealing himself as the miles flew by the windows either side of the truck.

Slowly working his way up to it, the man had eventually regaled the traveler with one lurid, hideous story after another about victims he'd abducted over the past twenty years—most of them young female prostitutes he'd picked up at a series of truck stops—used in a variety of obscene or disgusting ways, and then murdered and discarded along the nation's interstate highways, keeping a few small objects, jewelry, even body parts, as mementos, carefully hidden away in his truck.

At one point, he even displayed some of his terrible trophies to the traveler, who came closer to being sickened by them than might have been imagined. It had quickly, graphically, become apparent that the maniac had murdered men as well as women, and boys as well as girls.

Unlike the unfortunates on the man's long list of victims, the traveler had sought the driver out, virtually coerced him to provide transportation. But the traveler suffered no illusion that the killer was not preparing to broaden his *modus operandi*. No doubt he told these gory tales to all of his victims as a grisly substitute for foreplay.

In the end, the traveler had offered to compensate the driver for the ride by paying for an inexpensive room in their destination city, Memphis, which they could share for the night before they parted company the next morning. The driver hesitated, well outside of his "comfort zone." This was not going at all the way he had planned. But in the end, he had accepted. Adding to his collection of keepsakes—and his memories—was his highest priority, and this one should be easy.

Entering the city, the traveler had been interested by the number of signs directing tourists to many places historically associated with a variety of mysterious entities: Muddy Waters, Carl Perkins, Johnny Cash, W.C. Handy, B.B. King, Howlin' Wolf, Isaac Hayes. Yet even the traveler knew enough about Elvis Presley to realize that this place could be even worse—if that was possible—than Salzburg or Vienna.

The driver had dropped his container load off at a distribution center on the outskirts of town, and they had taken the tractor with them into downtown Memphis. The grandly-named Imperial Arms was a rundown transient men's hotel in a seedy area of the city. Parking in the alley—at the insistence of the management—they had walked up two flights of rickety, whitewashed, exterior stairs and found their room.

The key was turned in an obsolescent non-electronic lock.

The traveler had entered behind the driver. The instant the lock snapped, the man whirled without words, or any other preliminary, and struck out with a large knife. The traveler decided to teach the man a lesson of sorts and allowed the long, straight, double-edged dagger blade to sink deeply into the abdomen, fully to the hilt, which the traveler noticed resembled a large set of old-fashioned cast brass knuckledusters.

First World War, the traveler thought, *if I recall correctly. The American army*. It burned where it penetrated almost to the spine, but the traveler had felt far worse in the past, and almost enjoyed the sensation.

The man's eyes widened with astonishment and fear, especially after he twisted the knife and sawed it back and forth, from side to side in the wound, producing no visible effect on the part of the traveler, who casually seized his wrist in a crushing, painful grip, pushed the hand and knife away, and then seized the driver by the throat.

With casual effort, the traveler turned the truck driver ninety degrees, then walked him backwards into the tiny, badly-lit bathroom, where he stumbled over the edge of the tub and fell—held up only by the traveler's grip on his throat—pulling the plastic curtains down from their rod as he landed on his back on the musty-smelling non-slip mat.

Somehow, the bloodied knife changed hands.

"Noooooo!" the driver screamed, only to be stifled by a cruel and implacable hand. Methodically, and without visible emotion of any kind, the traveler cut him—the knife was so dull it hurt terribly—either side of his neck, into each armpit, up through the abdomen where a heavy artery hides behind the stomach, and then twice more at the femoral arteries in the groin. Before he lost consciousness and expired, the driver understood exactly what the traveler had done to him.

He had done it himself, to so many others.

There would be no blood feast here, thought the traveler, washing up in the sink. The victim was tainted—morally—and the idea was repulsive.

Instead, the traveler would rest until dusk—this sunblock was becoming a burdensome annoyance but cleaning up was impossible now, the shower was occupied and the curtains had been torn down—feed, obtain some other form of transportation (perhaps it would be pleasant to drive an automobile on these highways) and continue on to the next destination.

Another step closer to closure, after all these years.

5: "*ALLONS ENFANTS...*"

"Evil to him who thinks evil of it."—King Edward III of England

*M*otto of the Order of the Garter
The blood feeds the virus, not the vampire.

Not without a fight, the Germans were finally driven out of our little village. For a couple of days it was very noisy outside, and a wine cellar was a good place even if it hadn't contained a beautiful, willing girl and all the wine in the world. Artillery tends to be like that.

I felt like a coward and a fool for not doing anything, well, military, until Surica asked me what I thought I could accomplish against a couple of thousand Nazis, with a .45 caliber pistol and twenty-two rounds of ammunition. Her service piece was even sillier, a Romanian-issue .380 caliber Beretta Model 1934 with two seven-round magazines and one up the spout, a badge of rank more than anything else.

Still don't feel quite right about it, though. Who died because I wasn't there to plug a Nazi in the back, the guy who might have cured Alzheimer's?

She told me that her full name was Surica Fieraru, and that she was a fighter pilot from the Free Romania movement, the Smaranda Braescu squadron (whatever that meant), flying escort out of England for the enormous fleets of B-17s and B-24s that were bringing the war back to Hitler. She'd taken severe anti-aircraft fire coming back from her latest mission and screwed her little purloined IAR 80A into the ground in a forest a few miles away from the town we were now hiding in.

Any landing you walk away from, as the saying goes. She walked pretty well, I thought, once I could see her. But I'm getting ahead of myself.

All those weeks together, Surica and I didn't have much to speak of in the way of food—a little canvas shoulder bag of dreaded K-rations, two days' worth, six little waxed cardboard boxes exactly the size of a Cracker Jack package, was all that I'd brought to the picnic and she had even less—but we certainly did have plenty of wine.

And each other.

We had a couple of different buzzes going all the time—at least I did—one alcoholic, the other sexual. I never really noticed when all of the usual stuff—and some pretty damned unusual stuff, as well: 24-year-old farm kids from east central Illinois (and their temporary send-off girlfriends) didn't have a clue about sex in 1944—began to be supplemented with some provocative and exciting biting and bloodletting. A lot less of the latter than you'd think. Like I said, the blood is for the virus. By the time it all started, it only seemed right and proper—logical, somehow, and sexy as hell—and it didn't hurt even a little. Before long, I got as good at it as she was.

There is no taste in the world like that of fresh blood to a vampire. The blood is for the virus, but the virus makes the effort worthwhile.

One thing that bothered me, at first, was the absolute darkness. Because it was uncomfortable to ride with it on my pistol belt, I'd left my flashlight in the Jeep that had taken off without me when the *Wehrmacht* made their appearance in the little town. We had felt around for candles. No joy. My rations had contained matches, but I didn't smoke, and I'd foolishly traded them off, along with all of the little four-cigarette packages that came with each meal, for more chocolate.

"You need to see my face that badly?" Surica would ask, pretending (or maybe not pretending) to be hurt. "But what will you do if I am ugly?"

I knew that she wasn't ugly, although I'm not entirely certain that it would have mattered. By then, my fingers knew her face as well as they knew the rest of her. She had a lovely broad, smooth forehead, flawless velvet skin, slightly arched symmetrical brows, eyes that somehow felt eastern European—hard to tell by touch, potentially painful—high, prominent cheekbones, a good, straight nose, not quite turned up, lush, full lips, especially the lower one, and a little squared-off chin. Not a single scar, wart, or hairy mole to be counted. Surica's teeth were perfect, nice and straight, punctuated by that pair of elongated upper canine incisors that no longer surprised me.

I could feel my own beginning to grow.

As for the rest of her, Surica was everything that any 24-year-old kid from east central Illinois could have wished for, and more: long-legged, slender-waisted, with narrow hips—my mother, a farm wife ever mindful of the importance of baby-making, would probably have disapproved—a rather small backside shaped like a perfect upside-down heart, and those amazing baubles below her collarbones. Surica made me feel like it was my birthday and Christmas all at the same time.

About the way she smelled: she didn't really have a scent, it just felt wonderful inhaling close to the hollow of her neck, maybe like extra oxygen. A couple of decades from now they would start calling it pheromones. For now, it just added to the amazing rush of being with her.

Then, after a week or so had gone by, I woke up (you can't really say "one morning" when you don't have a clue what time it is) to discover that I didn't need candles or matches or flashlights any more. It no longer seemed dark in our wine cellar (I realized, of course, that Surica had been able to see me from the very beginning) but just as brightly lit as my mother's kitchen on a school day morning.

She was more beautiful than my fingers had told me she was, though by then, it may have been the virus talking. She had red hair, deep red, almost maroon. I never knew eastern Europeans could have red hair.

"So you can finally see, my love," she breathed. "Welcome to a new world."

A bleak moment. I'd probably seen more than my share of vampire movies, although there were a lot fewer then than there seem to be these days. Aside from worrying about becoming a sniveling Renfield (was I getting hungry enough to scrounge around for bugs?), I had another concern. "How many others have you done this to?" We had been sort of squatting on the floor, side by side, backs to one of the many wine racks. I rose, now, not really knowing what I wanted to hear her say.

"I think I recall that you did it to yourself, my love, and with considerable enthusiasm. As to how many before you...a lady doesn't tell, and I assure you, I am a lady. I am of a passionate disposition, to be sure, but I am selective. I have had time to learn discretion, restraint. I was born in Romania, you see, not far from the Serbian border, in the year 1711, and I was 'brought over' when I was only seventeen."

My new girlfriend was older than me. Two hundred nine years older.

Still crouching, she looked up at me from under lowered eyelashes. I was looking straight down into her open collar, and it was a hell of a sight. "Would you believe me if I said you are the first person I have ever brought over?" She reached seductively for the fly of my trousers.

I grinned, nodding my head. "I will, dear Surica, if you want me to. Do you want me to?"

But by then, of course, she couldn't answer.

6: SHOTS IN THE DARK

"Among the other causes of evil that being unarmed brings you, it makes you contemptible."—Niccolo Machiavelli

The Hamilton County shooting range northwest of town consists of half a dozen lanes that accommodate six or eight shooters, separated by barrows, or berms pushed up out of the Bentonite soil with a bladed caterpillar. The gate locks, and civilians aren't allowed to use it in the dark. I once asked a county commissioner about that, and I think I saw his hair turn white right there on the spot, just thinking about liability.

The New Prospect police are required to practice under low light conditions, since that's when most violent crime happens to get committed.

I picked Anton up at his home at eight o'clock, wondering about how things had turned out with his wife. As he loaded a couple of cased long guns and his shooting bag into the back of the car, he told me without being asked, that Priscilla was being held over at the hospital for another night. Their son Patrick was home from the Air Force Academy, owing to his mother's illness, and was keeping her company. Their daughter was coming back from Vermont as quickly as she could.

I knew Anton wanted desperately to be with Priscilla. I would have in his place. But he absolutely had to go to the range—or do something else that involved plenty of sound and fury—or his heart would burst from the terror and despair that he was unaware he reeked of.

It was an unusually warm evening, the drive east, out onto the prairie, very pleasant. With the windows down, I could smell a world of coyotes, foxes, deer, prairie dogs, burrowing owls, other winged predators most folks don't know about except from TV nature programs. The sky was clear and there was no Moon. I could have turned the headlights off and driven by starlight, but it would have aggravated Anton.

We pulled up to the steel pipe gate. He got out and unlocked it. I drove through. He relocked it and climbed back up into the Suburban. We jounced over a rutted road until we reached the part of the range we wanted. There didn't appear to be anybody else around this evening. I turned the machine around and backed up to the line of shooting benches.

I try to avoid violence whenever I can, if only because it doesn't pay a person like me to be conspicuous. If you can run 40 miles an hour, leave finger dimples in bricks, and punch holes in cinderblocks barefisted (I have to admit that hurts a little), it isn't much of a problem. I've been shot more than once and gotten over it the next day.

But I keep a couple of guns around, just in case. One is the .45 auto the Army issued me in 1942. The other is a Colt, as well, a .38 caliber Detective Special I confiscated from a sap who shot me with it in Lubbock, Texas, in 1969. Was he ever surprised when I didn't fall down as he'd expected, but broke his nose and took his gun. I let him escape.

Oh, and I have a shotgun, too, a Remington Model 870 with what's called a "riot barrel," an extended six-shot magazine, and rifle sights, that I can reload shells for when Anton and I go shooting claybirds.

There was some light provided at the range, of course, the old-fashioned blue-green style, set up on telephone-like wooden posts, approximating the street lights in the older, quieter parts of town. I'm not sure that the effect was intentional, but it was useful. I've always disliked the newer reddish-brown street lighting. It's ugly and depressing.

I would have been okay without any artificial light, but Anton didn't know that, and he had too many other things to worry about just now.

Pulling his stuff out of the back of my car, he laid an old plaid wool blanket across the top of the concrete bench and set his gun bag down. He laid his long guns in their soft-sided zippered cases beside it.

I spread my long coat on the next bench to the left, set my .38 in its little plastic envelope on it, and my cased shotgun, as well. Then we took a staple gun and a stack of targets forward—we had chosen one of the 25-yard ranges although most real life and death pistol fighting happens at something more like three yards—and attached them to a couple of four-by-eight sheets of plywood, already so full of bullet holes, they almost weren't there. They were held up by four inch steel pipes concreted into the ground. You weren't supposed to shoot at the pipes, but they were pretty full of bullet holes of their own.

Both of us had violated strict range protocol, carrying our loaded sidearms downrange with us. To each of us they were like an article of clothing, more or less forgotten until they were needed. But Anton was a cop, with a badge and other credentials. Given the alternatives that portion of Colorado offers, between so-called "open carry" and begging for concealed carry permission, my personal choice is "Don't ask don't tell."

Back at the benches, each of us removed the magazines and chamber cartridges from the pistols we were carrying—my .45s were 230-grain Federal HydraShok, and the .40s Anton stuffed in his old Glock M22 were 155-grain Winchester SilverTips, both of them accurate, highly effective but expensive loads—and replaced them with magazines filled with cheaper practice ammunition, chosen to duplicate, more or less, the ballistic behavior of the "social" loads we carried every day.

Shooting glasses, ear protectors, ready on the right, ready on the left, ready on the firing line, *Fire!* And we did, with considerable satisfaction. Fourteen rounds for Anton before he ran dry and had to reload, eight for me, leaving one in the chamber so I wouldn't have to work the slide to get shooting again. I've urged Anton many times to count his shots so he might enjoy the same tactical advantage. He replies, in a real firefight, you've got other things on your mind, and he's got a point. I'm in less danger and can take a more relaxed view.

Each time we fired, blue and pink fireballs 18 inches in diameter blossomed just forward of the muzzles of our pistols. You could have read a newspaper by them, if you'd been an Evelyn Wood graduate. Brass clinked merrily on the concrete walkway connecting the benches and the hardened clay either side of it. Gouts of dust billowed on the earthen berm behind the targets. The night birds even shut up for a little while.

And there is no perfume like the smell of burned smokeless powder.

We were in no hurry. I usually carry two spares—the eight-shot re-engineered magazines work perfectly in my Colt—so at 25 rounds, I was finished. Anton only carries one 13-round spare, so he was done at 27. He looked over at me, grinning like a little kid from ear to ear as he invariably does. He nodded toward the targets and I nodded back, so we removed our dusty plastic glasses and sweaty ear protectors and walked up front to inspect the holes we'd just made in five pieces of paper.

Hey, it isn't any sillier than golf.

Anton had a 14-round group on his first target (magazine plus chamber) and a 13-round group on the other. Every hole lay within the outermost ten-inch circle, most of them in an inner three-inch circle, centered may-be an inch high and a little to the right. Given the poor lighting—not to mention what was going on inside him—it was more than acceptable. No sane individual would want Anton Varick mad at him.

I'd put an eight-shot magazine into each of three targets, saving the chamber round by habit. (It had popped out in my hand when I'd cleared the gun to come forward.) Each target showed a single ragged hole an inch and a half in diameter, centered perfectly. Mediocre shooting for me, but when he saw them, Anton whistled, as he always does. He says I'm a wizard. He doesn't know that the truth—inhuman strength, telescopic nocturnal vision—is a whole lot weirder than that.

We repeated the exercise a couple of times. I fired three six-shot cyl-inders of .38 Special from my little Colt revolver. Anton won't carry a backup, says it's against department policy (which it isn't—I looked it up—it's against Anton Varick policy). I once gave him a little .40 caliber derringer, from Waco, Texas, but he never carries it.

Priscilla does.

Then we limbered up our shotguns, his Winchester, mine Remington, using solid slugs instead of birdshot, the latter being much too hard on the range's poor, abused plywood backboards. Even most shooters don't understand that slugs put the family 12 gauge high among the ranks of the good old African elephant guns a saner generation of Englishmen treasured. It's the "nuclear option" of America's household arsenal.

I put seven fat slugs into a big mutant cloverleaf-shaped hole. Anton's group was actually smaller than mine. It made us both happy. Having ti-died up behind us, targets in the trash, brass "policed" for later use, Anton was a different man when he climbed back into the car.

"Giff, what do you say I buy you a drink?"

"I say, yippee!" Inwardly, I groaned a bit. I knew where we were headed. Bryce's Bar, in Otomy, Colorado.

Home (one of them, anyway) of the Rocky Mountain Oyster.

THE TRAVELER: TULSA, OKLAHOMA

"Evil is done without effort, naturally, it is the working of fate;
good is always the product of an art."—Charles Baudelaire

According to information that the traveler had sought and found online at an Internet cafe in Memphis, the most common car being driven in America these days was a ten-year-old silver-gray Toyota Corolla.

Having seriously considered purchasing or renting a conveyance and rejecting the idea—money was no problem, but the seller or renter would certainly have required more information than the traveler was willing to surrender—the best solution seemed to be to find such a car parked where it could easily be stolen. The city seemed to have an unusual number of colleges and universities, and their parking lots seemed to abound with ten-year-old silver-gray Toyota Corollas, owned no doubt by impoverished students, parked beside Lexuses, Porsches and BMWs.

Rich kids, spending Daddy's money—or tenured faculty members.

In a relatively short time, the traveler came across an acceptable vehicle, unlocked it with a simple device—commonly called a "slim jim"—from the canvas bag, cheated the ignition lock (a skill the traveler had been perfecting almost since the time of Henry Ford), and drove it to another college lot nearby, where another ten-year-old silver-gray Toyota Corolla waited patiently to exchange license plates.

Stopping at a McDonald's on the way out of town—the food was convenient and reasonably palatable and so was the counter girl the traveler trapped in a bathroom stall and allowed to live afterward, without remembering, as a sort of gratuity—the Toyota's wheels soon turned westward. The traveler tried to find something on the radio besides so-called "country music" but was disappointed. When the device found a rare rap station on the dial, the traveler turned it off.

○

Dawn found the traveler entering a place called Tulsa, Oklahoma. This region of North America had always looked like a desert on maps, but it was almost lush, thickly grown with vegetation both accidental and deliberate. The air was full of vegetable odors and those of all kinds of animals. Most human beings would probably find the whole thing extremely pleasant. It made the traveler want to seek some tall building, crowded about with other tall buildings, where humans were crammed together and kept helpless and vulnerable by predators vastly more voracious and implacable than any vampire could be: their own governments.

Perhaps it was time to spend some money—and maybe to acquire another car. The traveler steered the Toyota toward the tallest buildings and found a first-rate hotel. Leaving the car in a parking garage underground—carefully, every camera was noted and mentally charted—the traveler took some time deciding what kind of car to drive next, made a tentative decision, and then went upstairs to the lobby.

The transaction for a room was made in cash, of which the traveler possessed an abundance. In these security-conscious times—some few might have called it a police state; the traveler was well acquainted with those—a driver's license or some other sort of photographic identification was required. The traveler quietly suggested that the clerk use her own; she happily agreed. Once the I.D. had been scanned, she handed a keycard to a nearby bellboy who took the only luggage the traveler carried, the canvas shoulder bag, leading the way to the elevators.

At the room, the traveler followed the bellboy in, accepted the keycard, and, as the young man held his hand out for a tip, caught his eye. As it often was, there was a second's confusion on the subject's part.

"Shut the door, please," ordered the traveler, turning on the television to cover up the noise of a struggle in case the victim proved unexpectedly difficult to control. It had happened, on occasion.

"Sure thing." Satisfaction. The boy would be no trouble at all.

The blood was calling out loudly, shrilly to the traveler as it sometimes did; it had been a while since feeding, although far worse privation had been endured. But some discretion was obviously called for.

"Please take your jacket off."

The bellboy complied. "Might there be something else I can do for you?"

"As a matter of fact," replied the traveler and sank a pair of incisors into the young man's pulsing throat. They stood like that for a moment, until the traveler was able to stop—it became difficult sometimes. Then the bellboy's quickly-healing wounds were cleaned up with a damp paper towel from the little kitchenette area, and his unbloodied uniform jacket was replaced. Its high collar would conceal the puncture marks until, thanks to the traveler's potent saliva, they faded.

The traveler handed the young man a twenty dollar bill, pushing him a little. It didn't require much effort. "I'd appreciate it if you would forget everything that just happened in this room, except the tip."

The boy looked at the twenty. "Gee, thanks! Always happy to be of service!"

○

Having taken a long, restorative shower, rinsed out every item in an admittedly limited wardrobe, and left them to dry in front of the air conditioner, blasting away on high, and in the fan-ventilated bathroom, the traveler slept naked and serene through most of the day. Then, dressing in clean clothes, shouldering the canvas bag, and taking an elevator straight to the parking garage was quick and simple.

The car the traveler had selected earlier was still there, an elderly blue Camaro in fairly good condition with a National Rifle Association sticker on what served as its back bumper. The car's principal attraction was that it happened to be sitting in what appeared to be a blind spot between two security cameras set a little too far apart. The car was old enough not to have a security circuit, so the door was opened easily and the engine was turning over in a moment.

The first stop, after having the car washed and vacuuming it out thoroughly—it had been full of some student's books and other junk that had to be thrown away—was a big parking lot elsewhere in town where the traveler failed to find another blue Camaro, but saw a blue Pontiac Firebird of about the same age that might be mistaken for a Camaro. Plates were exchanged, as they had been in Memphis, and the traveler was off toward the western edge of Tulsa, for a meal and to feed.

A young would-be car thief the traveler had lured by leaving the Firebird running at Arby's was found in an unfinished subdivision—the economy again—snagged by a branch, floating in the Arkansas River.

7: *COJONES*

"Boredom is the root of all evil."—Soren Kierkegaard

*B*ack into the night, we headed away from New Prospect, not toward it. Northern Colorado, east of Interstate 25, used to be rural for the most part, but these days it's filling up with light at a frenetic pace.

On the other hand, when I was born in 1920, the United States population was one sixth of what it is now, but you couldn't drive around the corner for a cheeseburger or taco, and there was nothing on TV.

There are always trade-offs.

Otomy, halfway between I-25 and US 85, out on County Road 23, is supposed to be an Indian—pardon me, "Native American"—name, but, given the specialty of the house at the little town's principal bar and grill, it seemed to me that its surgical implications were more appropriate.

Anton was like a different guy for our trip to the range, although I was well aware that the apparent change was mostly temporary. Sooner or later, he'd need to get back to his Priscilla, mortally ill as she was, back to being Chief of Detectives, and the weight of the world would settle on his weary shoulders again. But at least he'd had this evening.

I'd been there, myself, although the circumstances hadn't been nearly as dire. The night of the 1968 Democratic national convention in Chicago—where I happened to be living at the time; it was the closest I'd come geographically to the tiny farming community in which I'd been born, and from which I'd taken my *nom de guerre*, in almost a quarter of a century—the damn cops made me so mad that I went down in the basement of the house where I lived in Lincoln Park (and a previous tenant had thoughtfully left huge bales of old newspapers I used as a backstop) and burned up four boxes of .45 ACP. No ear protection: the virus defends my ears, repairing any damage I might do them.

It had helped a lot. I was able to go back to work (I was a private security consultant in those days), no longer shaking with rage. That year's candidate, Hubert Humphrey, resembled Porky Pig so strongly that I always expected to see him with a curly tail and no pants.

When we pulled up at Bryce's, the tiny, odd-shaped gravel lot was filled with more fancy road iron than a Harley-Davidson dealer. It didn't bother me, particularly. Most bikers are perfectly decent folks. Even when they're not, their blood—after the virus deals with any drugs or diseases it discovers—is just as good as anybody else's.

As we clambered out of the Suburban, I watched Anton readjust the holster on his belt and cover it with his jacket. It's always a good thing to be ready, just ask the Boy Scouts. In any case, the man just plain looked like a cop, no matter what he did. Take away his gun, his badge, and all of his clothing. What would you have? A naked cop. He didn't really try to hide it on this occasion, which was also a good thing. Anton thought going undercover meant turning his baseball cap around.

It could be embarrassing, sometimes.

We needn't have worried. Inside, sixty knights of the open road (or is that hoboes—I always forget) and their old ladies appeared to be celebrating the birthday of somebody's four-year-old daughter. A dozen rug-rats and anklebiters in Levis, miniature Harley Ts, tiny black leather vests, and paisley do-rags, were running around with cake on their faces. It's an increasingly strange world that we live in.

The place was long and narrow, with an oval bar down the center, the shape dictated by the plot of land it occupied, squeezed between the town's main street and the nearby river. The ceiling was low, and obscured by smoke despite the prissy preferences of the Colorado legislature. Someday, somebody's going to find a way to organize smokers as a voting block, and the political world will never be the same. The jukebox was blaring out "Let Freedom Ring," which I've always found stirring, even though it's about divorce, rather than politics.

The next song was "All My Exes Live in Texas." Perfect.

We found a Formica table in a dim corner and sat. Before too long, a harried-looking waitress in tight cutoffs and a nice little black midriffy top came to record our order for posterity. The constant harassment, sexual and otherwise, of the motorcycle class she could take, but a dozen small, noisy children appeared to be grinding her down. Two big helpings of Rocky Mountain Oysters, some raw veggies with ranch dressing to go with them, Negra Modelo for me, Fat Tire for Anton.

To tell a fundamental truth, it rarely gets better than that.

She carded me, of course. Eighty-nine years old and I still get carded. Surica brought me over when I was 24. I looked younger than that, although the way it really works is that the virus decides what your genetically optimal age is, was, or will be, and modifies you to suit. I've read horrifying medieval accounts of children—little babies—growing up overnight after being bitten. Not a very pleasant idea.

I don't carry a driver's license and I never have. I don't have a Private Investigator's license, either, or a concealed carry permit for my pistol and revolver. (If I have a Social Security number, I've long since forgotten what it was and so has the rest of the universe.) Instead, I slipped my hand inside my coat, withdrew it, and showed the waitress an empty palm. Anton watched it happen, but he saw the same thing she did. "Okay, honey," she said, "I'll get those beers right up."

And she did.

Anton held his glass up. "Nice to think they make this stuff only a few miles from where we live. I've always meant to take the New Belgium brewery tour." He took a long drink, and I concentrated on my lovely dark Mexican beer, which is also made at a small brewery, south of the border. Some places had it on draft, but you could only get it in bottles at Bryce's, which was a damn shame. "Here's to Fort Collins."

"Fort Collins," I repeated Anton's toast. Nice place. I had business there from time to time. Younger natives call it "Fort Funky." Robert Anton Wilson and Robert Shea readers call it "Fnord Collins."

Our "oysters" arrived at that moment, and we dug in. Fried just right, for the uninitiated, they are what make the difference between a bull and a steer. Removing them encourages the animal to concentrate on generating steaks, rather than on the cows in the next pen. The splendid snack the process provides us with is only a byproduct. They come in sheep and turkey flavor, too, and no, they do not taste like chicken.

We talked about this and that, avoiding the topic of Anton's wife. He wanted to know what I thought about putting some glow-in-the-dark tritium sights on his Glock. I allowed as how it might be a good idea. To be polite, I asked him about his AR-15, which he'd brought with him but hadn't shot. It had all the bells and whistles: a red-dot slightly telescopic sight, built-in flashlight, high-tech sling, Little Orphan Annie secret decoder ring, and this thing in the stock that tells time.

Too cluttered for my taste.

There was one small incident at Bryce's Bar that night, when I got up to go to the bathroom. The men's room door, when I exited the facilities, bumped into some guy on the other side of it who didn't seem to be a part of the natal day festivities, and he didn't take it kindly.

"Wash wear yer goin', Zorro!" I reasoned that his clever literary reference was to my hat, which I probably should have left in the Suburban. I'd more or less forgotten I was wearing my long coat and floppy chapeau, though I don't really need them after dark. I thought they made me look more like a Lamont Cranston than a Don Diego de la Vega.

There wasn't enough room to change your mind in the dark, tiny corridor that led to the men's room, straight ahead, and the women's on the right. His back to the main room, he raised a drunken fist to collarbone level where only I could see it. "I'll make you a new face!"

With that, he threw a short jab, which I caught and held, trying not to crush his hand. Someday he might be sober again and a decent guy. Or not. His do-rag was leather. His stubbly face had more craters than the back of the Moon. His breath was a violation of the Geneva Convention.

"You don't want to do that at a kiddies' birthday party, do you?" I pushed him as hard as the powers I possessed would let me. His face softened. He looked guilty. "I have a better idea: why don't you pee yourself?"

Which he did, then and there.

It probably wasn't the first time.

I went back to the table and ate some more bull's testicles.

8: NIGHT MOVES

"It is in the solitary mind and soul of the individual that the battle between good and evil is waged and ultimately won or lost."—M. Scott Peck

*W*e got back into town just before midnight, driving past the chain motels, bars, all-night coffee shops, and diners. New Prospect night life.

Toward the center of the town, Anton said, "Please drop me off at the hospital, will you Giff? If you don't mind. Patrick has his mom's Cherokee just now. We'll come over and pick up my car and long guns tomorrow."

"That'll do." I mustn't hesitate. "Can I come up and see Priscilla now?" I'd been thinking hard about this since Anton had told me the news.

Anton looked a little surprised. "I didn't realize you'd want to, Giff. It's not fun. But if she's awake, she'd love to see you, I'm sure."

We parked in an almost empty lot. This time I left my hat in the Suburban, but took my long coat for the contents of its pockets. I'd made my decision on the way back from Bryce's. Priscilla, after all, was my friend, and the love of my best friend's life. She had accepted me into her family. I was not just going to sit around and watch her die.

One certainty that nine decades have taught me: despite the lofty declarations made by those who can only theorize and won't have any choice to make about it, I will never get tired of living; for all of its faults and hazards, life offers far too many pleasures, far too many satisfactions, far too many joys and delights, to just let it slip away without a fight. After my millionth slice of lemon meringue pie, I'll look forward to my million and first. And if the Grim Reaper ever comes for me, the bastard's going to require serious medical attention.

If I brought Priscilla over—a choice I'd really rather not have to make for her—if I inadvertently made her into a vampire like me, then I would deal with it, under the same general rule as the one that says it's better to do something you believe is necessary, and have to apologize for it, than to ask permission and get turned down. They both might end up hating my guts, but Anton would have his Priscilla, alive.

Not dead, not undead, not even partially dead, but alive.

It's a virus, remember?

"Stairs or elevator?" Anton asked me. Usually, he was a big fan of what I regarded as gratuitous exercise. I shrugged, so we took the elevator. They had her up on the oncology floor, of course, one of the weirdest, nastiest-smelling places in New Prospect. Even those without my olfactory acuity notice it. It isn't anybody's fault, it's just ugly. Might have been part of what Anton had meant by its being not fun.

Patrick was waiting for us (Anton had called ahead), sitting by the bed, holding his mother's hand. He stood, hugged his dad for a long moment, tears starting in his eyes. Shaking them off, he took my hand with both of his. Light blond like his mother, he was tall and lean, better looking than his old man, better muscled than he had been before the Academy—wearing his uniform, probably for his mother. He looked like a recruiting ad for the Master Race but that wasn't his fault.

Patrick had regarded me as his uncle all his life. I had been the family sitter over the years, had taken him and his sister to play miniature golf (at night, of course), to the batting cages in the park—he pitched for the Academy, now—occasionally bowling, and to the movies.

"Hello, J!" Priscilla smiled up at me from the bed. She looked terrible: thin, strained, more silver in that shining cap of gold than I had ever seen before. I suddenly realized that I knew this woman better—or at least I'd known her longer—than any other female in my life. I'd known Priscilla almost exactly as long as I'd known my mother.

She had deep, dark circles all the way around her eyes, at the moment, and was having some difficulty breathing, despite the transparent oxygen line crawling across her upper lip. I looked to Anton and his son, then I perched on the edge of the bed and took her hand.

"Don't talk if it's hard for you, Priscilla. I'm happy just to see you smile. You're gonna beat this, I promise, no matter what the docs say."

Behind me, I heard twin gasps, whether at the promise or my hubris making it, I didn't know. I did know that I had to get rid of them for about fifteen minutes, and I didn't want to erase their memories. Far easier to send them away. They couldn't remember what they hadn't seen.

"Why don't you two guys go down to the cafeteria. The kitchen's almost certainly closed, but they'll have a lot of stuff in machines, and I know they keep a great big kettle of fresh coffee going all the time. It's not too bad. In fact you can bring me some when you come back up. I'll keep Priscilla company. You guys would probably like to talk."

I pressed a little with those last few words. They blinked, then nodded at the unassailable logic of it. "We'll be right back, baby," Anton told his wife. I stood up and got out of his way so he could bend over the bed and kiss her. Then he and Patrick went out the door and headed for the elevator. I could hear Patrick telling his dad that his sister Amber would be taking a shuttle bus from the airport in Denver.

I shut the door behind them, reached for my blood kit in my coat, which I'd draped over a chair, and looked Priscilla in her weary eyes. She had been pretty. She would be again. "Tired, aren't you? Bet you'd like to sleep. Let go of your pain and worry. Take a nice nap. Don't wake up again until I ask you to. By then, the guys will be back, okay?"

She nodded weakly and shut her eyes. When her breathing was right, I pulled out one of my fifty-microliter syringes, used an alcohol wipe on myself, and drew blood, which I immediately injected into her right carotid artery. I would rather have used the femoral, but the needle wasn't long enough. I was getting ready to repeat the procedure with her left carotid, when the door opened suddenly. In it, stood a young nurse.

"What are you doing?" the girl demanded in a horrified tone. Like many another nurse, she smelled of fresh coffee and violet-scented handsoap. Like many another nurse, she would weigh two hundred and fifty pounds before she turned thirty. I've never figured that one out.

She also had a cat. Siamese.

I looked over my shoulder and went on getting ready to draw more blood. "Please, nurse, just stand there and be quiet. What's your name?"

She blinked. Her eyes were big and almost black. "I...I'm Consuelo."

"That's a pretty name, Consuelo." Another thing I've never figured out is why a Mexican girl's name has a masculine ending. "I'm J," I said. "Just a letter, not an initial. When I was born, my folks couldn't agree whether to call me John or James, so my birth certificate reads 'J'."

Even after 65 years, I still don't know much about this persuasion thing. I know it helps to be as matter-of-fact and conversational as possible.

"Why don't you turn around, stand there in the door, and let me know if anybody else heads in this direction. Will you please do that, Consuelo?"

She smiled, and it was like the sun coming out. "I'd be happy to, J!"

I finished with the draw, then applied another swab to Priscilla's neck, and injected a second half cc of my blood. This was completely unexplored territory to me, and it was all I dared to use this first time around. Maybe I'd use more later on. "Mrs. Varick's going to get better now, Consuelo. If she doesn't, if she gets worse, you call me right away. My phone number is..." And I told her. "Don't forget it. But don't remember any of this unless she gets sicker again, and then only the number—and the fact that you're supposed to call me, all right?"

The puncture mark would be undetectable in five minutes, gone in ten.

She smiled at me again. "All right, Doctor."

"Not doctor, just a friend. I'm J," I reminded her, putting my blood kit away. I was tempted to tell her that if she could manage to lose half a pound a week for the next year and a half, she could be the prettiest, slenderest nurse in the whole hospital. But she knew that.

"Okay, J." She smiled and I let her go.

THE TRAVELER: WICHITA, KANSAS

"The pious pretense that evil does not exist only makes it
vague, enormous and menacing."—Aleister Crowley

*H*ard times had come sweeping down over the Grand Prairie, just as they had on many occasions before this, and doubtless would someday again.

This time, it was the empty parking lots at shopping malls and downtown, the shuttered storefronts, and the abandoned businesses that told a story of political incompetence and economic disaster (another age, it might have been deserted farms), along with unfilled potholes and crumbling curbs that added an epilogue of civic despair all their own.

This town had been an historic, all-important hub for the westward movement of Americans in the 19th century. Cattle from Texas had been herded here to meet the railroad. For a while it had been a center for the manufacture of aircraft. For an interesting hour or two before sunrise, the traveler explored the streets of Wichita until the Firebird passed by a boarded-up national brand motel not far from the city's center.

It certainly presented possibilities, although the police would be watching the location to keep the homeless from squatting in the many rooms available here or from throwing trash into the emptied swimming pool, which at present had a tall, padlocked chainlink fence around it.

But one thing was certain: they would not be getting out of their safe, secure, heated, or air-conditioned patrol cars if they could avoid it. Gang signs, some of them oddly beautiful in a way, had been spray-painted on every vertical surface of the place, in their secret language claiming territory, making threats, exchanging insults. The traveler had seen it all many times before, in ancient times, on other continents.

It had started in the caves.

What the signs said, in language anyone could understand, was that this was not a safe place to walk down a street thinking of anything but walking down a street. It was a place to be alert—or somewhere else.

Hearing in Europe of the American version of this phenomenon had led the traveler to the opinion that every graffitist caught at the scene of his crimes ought to be killed outright—whether by police or private individuals was immaterial—not for his contempt for private property, but for the assault it represented on civilization itself.

On the other hand, the traveler reasoned, there was such a thing as freedom of artistic expression. Just think about Lascaux. Perhaps it was a value noble enough to die for, maybe even for an entire civilization to die for. And if everything should collapse tomorrow—as the traveler had thought it might on many previous occasions over the millennia—life would go right on for a vampire with very few significant changes, exactly as it had long before the dawn of human civilization.

On the next street over from the abandoned motel rose a four-story parking structure. For a nominal fee, the Firebird could be left there all night in relative safety. There were security cameras everywhere (although many of them seemed to be in a sorry state of disrepair), or the traveler might have dragged the attendant from her booth and fed then and there. Instead, the traveler walked from the car park to the abandoned motel. Instead of a room, the main building was selected, rather easily broken into, and secured again from the inside.

Although clean and relatively tidy, considering the fact that it had fallen into disuse, the lobby was completely unpromising for the traveler's purposes. Downstairs in the basement there was a large conference room, meant for corporate meetings and small conventions. Rows of folding tables—many still had tablecloths and carafes for drinking water—and folding metal chairs still occupied most of the space.

Best of all, there were no windows.

Although the electricity had long since been shut off—no one who could see perfectly in the dark would care about that—there was still running water in a kitchen-like facility that served the larger room, possibly owing to fire regulations, and the plumbing worked. The traveler could pass a day here in relative comfort and safety, resting, then resume the westward journey again, once darkness had fallen.

Only one thing remained before the traveler could sleep, and that was a brief exploration of the alley behind the motel in hopes of finding some derelict to feed from. Or perhaps some young person behind the counter in one of the seedy little gift shops across the street.

Slipping out of the motel again, and remaining in the shadows of the alley, it wasn't long before the traveler found a young woman taking her dog for a morning walk. It was a full-sized male poodle, its wooly coat uncut. The traveler didn't care much for dogs and never had.

Humans always seemed to have them around. They warned their masters and protected them from strangers—especially non-human strangers—which the traveler found inconvenient. They smelled bad, drooled, defecated, and urinated on everything in sight. But they fawned on their human masters, offering them what appeared to be unconditional love, which the humans returned abundantly. It was sickening.

The girl obviously intended to avoid eye contact with the traveler and pass by in the alley shadows without acknowledging another person's presence. Her dog had other ideas. Poodles have a reputation that demeans them, brought about by their silly name and the ridiculous (albeit utilitarian) way their fur is sometimes sculpted. They are intelligent, for dogs, fierce—they have been bred to hunt—and intensely loyal and protective to those they think of as their family.

The instant the traveler had appeared in the alley, the animal had reacted as if something in its genes had recognized an ancient enemy, baring its teeth, growling, rigid in a posture of threat display. When the traveler reached for the young woman, the poodle leapt for the adversary, and the vampire nearly lost control of the prey.

In one swift movement, the traveler seized the animal, twisted its head to break its neck, then took the girl, almost paralyzed with fear and grief, by her shoulders and spoke to her quietly for a minute or two.

Under rigid control, and following the traveler's commands, the girl lifted the body of her dead companion, carried it to a dumpster a few yards away, and without visible expression on her face—but with tears flooding down her cheeks—lifted the lid and threw the animal away.

They walked to the end of the alley, turned, and started for the abandoned motel. On the way, they passed an old woman breathing oxygen from a tube and using a wheeled walker. She noticed the young woman's tears.

"Are you all right, dear?" she asked, concern etching her wrinkled face.

The traveler answered, "Her dog just died."

The girl nodded and followed the traveler back to the motel.

Safe, secure shelter for the day, a dark, quiet, comfortable place to sleep until sunset—all those tablecloths together, clean on the side in contact with the tables, would make excellent bedding—a tasty "midnight" snack, and perhaps, with sufficient restraint, even breakfast.

The traveler had certainly fared worse over a long, eventful lifetime.

9: FRIENDS IN NEED

"Speak no evil, that thou mayest not hear it
spoken unto thee."—Bahá'u'lláh

*M*ornings and vampires don't mix. This vampire, anyway, I can't speak for others. I don't know any other vampires I could speak for. Except for lovely Surica, back in 1944, I've never met another vampire.

I've often wondered about that. But then I wonder about a lot. It's a desirable quality in a detective, I suppose, but it's also annoying.

This vampire doesn't seem to need much sleep, though. My theory is that, twenty-four hours a day, the virus takes care of the physical repair folks normally undergo in their sleep. What that leaves is whatever happens in the human mind during sleep. Science doesn't know what that is, but says that if it doesn't happen, you eventually die. Cats, they claim, deprived of Rapid Eye Movement sleep get odd lesions in their brains, a lesion supposedly epidemic in winos whom alcohol takes directly from the waking state to deep sleep without passing through REM.

Sorry, make that "homeless persons" or maybe even "homeless peroffspring."

I got up, drank my blood for the day—you don't want to hear this, but the virus makes it taste like everything wonderful you ever ate or drank, like the elixir of the gods—and started on some real breakfast: three eggs over medium, hash browns, refried black beans, on a huge flour tortilla (sometimes I fry it in a skillet, which makes it nicely crisp and bubbly), the whole thing smothered in green chili. Tabasco and Cholula to taste. *Huevos rancheros*, for the rancher with balls.

Fiddlestring will eat green chili gladly enough, provided it has plenty of little chunks of pork in it, but it makes him fart a lot, and he greatly prefers a can of smoked sardines in "spring water," mashed up with a fork. The damned things are good—lots of calcium; I often eat them myself— but unless I handle them just right (the secret is to put the empty can and lid into a Ziploc bag before throwing it in the trash), they screw up my sense of smell for hours afterward.

My kitchen is big and sunny and bright, white walls and ceiling, white cabinets, laminated birch furniture, and stainless fixtures. Ceramic tiled floor. I'd spent a fortune putting special glass in the windows that cut the ultraviolet down to what you'd expect from the bright light of a full moon, which is to say, nothing. It's a pleasant room.

I was halfway through my splendid *huevos* when at once there came a rapping, as of someone gently tapping, tapping at my back porch door. Only Quinn and someone more. I could hear them talking, and caught her scent. I arose from the counter, stepped onto the glassed-in porch, careful of the direct morning sunlight that was about to flood it, and turned a key that lives permanently in the old-timey lock.

Quinlan "Quinn" Kowalski stepped onto the porch as I made room for him. He needed room. Even in the world of professional wrestling, he'd been known as "Man Mountain Quinn," six foot three, 300 pounds, with long silver hair and a massive beard that made him look like the old fat Las Vegas Jesus. The man had worked his way through college and graduate school that way, had a PhD with oak leaf clusters in physics, and knew more about computers than any other sapient in the Known Universe.

He held a big carrying case I recognized.

Right behind Quinn came Tran Thi Thu-Quyen—also pronounced "Quinn"— his partner, confidant, lover, and, for all I knew, wife. A formidable mathematician, she was all of four-feet eleven inches, probably weighed 95 pounds soaking wet with a bottle of pop in each pocket, as Brother Dave Gardner used to say—or was it Justin Wilson? Strangers often took her for Quinn's adopted Vietnamese daughter.

They thought it was funny.

Quinn set the case down on the table, looked at my plate, then at the pans on the stovetop. "Mmm! Gay ranchero food! Got any to spare, J?"

"Stop that!" Quyen ordered with mock ferocity. To me: "We're on a diet just now—high protein liquids—um, different from yours." She sat down at the other end of the table, and Fiddlestring hopped up into her lap. In no time, he was purring loud enough to rattle the windows.

I nodded. "I understand. Make mine Clamato."

She giggled. Quinn and Quyen made a handsome living as freelance scientific consultants and expert trial witnesses—although Quinn took some delight in calling himself a "defrocked physicist." They probably knew more about me than I did, and a great deal of what I did know about being a vampire, I'd learned as a direct result of their research.

I'd met them several years ago when they went to buy a particular microscope and discovered that someone else—guess who—had bought the last one in the state. Not wanting to put their work on hold while another microscope got back-ordered, they'd persuaded the scientific supply outfit in Denver to call me and get permission for them to drop by.

In the end, they'd borrowed that microscope and other bits of equipment several times. (They were bringing it back again today.) We shared certain interests and a particular outlook on life. We'd visited, gone out together, and barbecued in their back yard and mine. They knew Anton's family—Quinn had tutored Patrick in computer science; his companion had done high school physics with Amber—and my cat was absolutely crazy about Quyen. They'd never bought my lame-assed stories about lupus or porphyria or whatever, and had guessed what it really was with me the third or fourth time we'd gotten together.

And kept their mouths shut.

To get it out of the way of conversation, I took the microscope into the spare bedroom I use as a study, and came back to find Quyen making a fresh pot of coffee. Quinn sat in her place, one pants leg pulled up, making adjustments to his prosthetic leg. He'd never told me what had cost him that leg, from the knee down, and I'd never asked, but he would squint one eye and make pirate noises from time to time.

He looked up at me now, and said, "Arrrrh!"

I sat, taking a steaming cup from Quyen when it was ready. I don't know how, but she made better coffee than I do with the same stuff. She sat at my right, between us. For a while we were silent. Suddenly Quinn said, "We need to talk to you about something. Ever sweep this room?"

I nodded toward the pantry. "Only with a broom," I answered.

Quinn grimaced. He felt that it was his job to make sorry jokes like that. Quyen grinned. He said, "You know perfectly well what I mean."

"I do. The place is clean." I meant it. If somebody had bugged my home and office, I would be able to smell their fingerprints on the devices—or the odor of their latex gloves—and possibly even hear the bugs working. I explained that to my friends and asked what was up.

"All right," said Quinn. "We had a visitor yesterday. Represented himself as working for a federal agency. He showed us a badge and ID, but I'm not sure if that means anything. He wanted to know all about you."

"*Moi*? What agency? What did he want to know?" I'd carefully avoided any kind of notoriety, and kept under the radar and off the grid as much as possible, for many years, so this was more than mildly unsettling. I'd paid what taxes I couldn't get out of through a dummy corporation.

"No Such Agen—" Quinn started.

Quyen stepped in. "How long have we known you. How well. What do you do for a living. How much money do you have. Who are your other friends. Do you have guns. Do you use drugs. Do you ever go out in the daylight."

That last question really made me worry.

It appeared that somebody knew I was a vampire.

10: IS IT SAFE?

"There are a thousand hacking at the branches of evil to one who is striking at the root."—Henry David Thoreau

"Okay, open wide. This won't take long."

He was right. It never did. And, although it was the silliest thing I was compelled to do from time to time, it was necessary for survival.

T.W. Beemort, D.D.S., ran a small dental practice within easy walking distance of my home, although I seldom walked there. I had chosen him, originally, because his building, a former residence, had a roof with a deep overhang. I could park under it and get through his door in just a few seconds, without having to expose myself to direct sunlight. Of such constraints, I reflected, is an individual's life composed.

T.W., I should explain, kept my fangs under control.

He was a big guy, heavily muscled, with sun-darkened forearms, and just about the shiniest bald head I've ever seen. I was always surprised that he didn't have any visible ink work. Or maybe an earring.

Despite his outward tough appearance, he was also the gentlest dentist who had ever worked on me, and probably the best educated and most literate. I didn't know what the man pursued as a hobby—his Muzak played 60s rock—or to stay in physical condition, but my guess was that it involved motorcycles, and maybe martial arts. He looked like a *sai* guy. I wondered if he ever visited Bryce's Bar in Otomy.

I never had any other dental problems. No tooth decay, no abscess-generating streptowhatsit stood a snowball's chance against the virus. I hadn't had a sore throat, a cold, or the flu since 1944. But my goddamn upper canine incisors just wouldn't stop growing until they were twice the length of those on either side. Sharp, too. If I left it too long, I'd end up nicking the tip of my tongue on them every time.

Your own blood doesn't do you any good, vampirewise.

I leaned back and tried to relax. The procedure never hurt, but the noise of T.W.'s handpiece, whirring through my enamel and dentine, up into my brainpan, never failed to remind me of that scene—you know the one—from *Marathon Man*. Dr. Mengele meets Tootsie. The enamel would reappear in couple of days. The rest of the tooth would start growing until I had to come back and see T.W. again in a few weeks.

Usually, we talked about books and movies—rather, he did, when my mug was full of dental equipment. Today, though, it was different. Through the noise of his micro-jackhammer, he said, "Somebody was in here asking after you yesterday afternoon. Somebody with government credentials."

"Rowrgh?" I replied, a little alarmed after Quinn and Quyen this morning.

"The trouble is, I happened to glance at a wall mirror in the waiting room, and his hand—which had seemed to hold his badge flipper and ID card, was empty in the mirror. I looked back, and they were there again. Then I looked in the mirror again and they were gone."

"Vernffle!" I attempted to exclaim.

"What does it mean, J? Can you tell me what it means?"

"Yurhnurngna—" I sat up and took the hose out of my mouth. I hadn't been anesthetized. "It means someone, someone like me—you know what that means—is checking me out. What did he want to know, T.W.?"

"Everything that I know—about you. I told him I didn't know you very well." Which was a lie. T.W. played poker every Thursday evening at my house, with Anton, Quinn, and Quyen. "He wanted to see your X-rays."

"Interesting. And you told him...?"

"To come back with a warrant. Sometimes I think I watch too much TV."

I hadn't known that, about phony vampire credentials in a mirror, but it was a good thing to have learned. I'd be more careful in the future.

If there *was* a future.

○

Greeley stinks.

There's no way to put it more politely than that. When the wind blows from a certain quarter, the smell of that city's world-famous feedlots—for both cattle and sheep, a deadly olfactory combination—can be overwhelming, even to those without a vampire's heightened sensibilities. Only worse thing I've ever smelled was a rendering plant.

And tannery.

I keep thinking about having a fancy new air conditioning system installed in the Suburban, with those super microfine filters you always hear about in vacuum cleaner commercials. Then the wind shifts, the awful smell goes away for a while and—just like the leaky roof in the Andrews Sisters' song *Mañana* once it's stopped raining—I forget.

The Andrews Sisters? Think of the McGuire Sisters in military—

The McGuire sisters? Okay, think of the Lennon Sisters, then.

The Lennon Sisters? Guess you had to be there.

Greeley lies about as far east of I-25 as New Prospect lies west, so that horrible smell travels about 40 miles to get here. People often complain about it. Politicians often threaten to *do something* about it. But I've never heard anybody complaining about their T-bone, their lamb chop, their nice woolen winter blanket, or their Cordoba, upholstered in fine Corinthian leather. It all kind of balances out, somehow.

Driving up the alley and pulling into the garage behind my house, beside the PT Cruiser, I waited for the big double door to come down before getting out of the car. It was much better in here; it only smelled of oil, gasoline, insecticides, weed killer, and bags of fertilizer.

I threw a couple of big bolts that locked the door down securely.

I don't know why it's become traditional for an attached garage to communicate with the house through a door in the kitchen. I've been in a few where that wasn't the case, but it was with mine, a fine old Arts and Crafts model built in the early 1920s on a quiet, tree-shaded street in one of the oldest neighborhoods in New Prospect. The garage had been added a couple of decades afterward and lay mostly behind the house.

Fine with me, less grass to mow. Hard enough to do as it is, in the dark, neighbors on both sides, also front and back, complaining. Given vampire strength I can use a non-powered mower, but I do it enthusiastically.

Extracting a small package from an inside pocket and laying it on the desk in my office, I took my hat and coat to the closet, and would have put a sweater on, like Mr. Rogers, to cover up my .45, except that I hadn't been carrying it that morning, not wanting to worry T.W.'s receptionist. But with what my dentist had just told me, on top of the news from Quinn and Quyen, I wouldn't be leaving home without it again until I knew why this faux fed was going around asking after me.

For now, having been greeted by Fiddlestring, and making sure his bowl was full—I keep dry food for him all the time, adding fishy snacks more or less randomly—I went upstairs to the bedroom where I keep my weapons, took my .38 from beside the .45, in a hidden drawer built into the bedframe, and dropped it into my right-hand front pants pocket.

Then I hurried back downstairs to the office.

I had an appointment with an important client.

THE TRAVELER: LEOTI, KANSAS

"An evil life is a kind of death."—Ovid

The stolen blue Firebird pulled into the tiny village of Leoti, Kansas, as a blush of false dawn began to paint the sky behind it. Windmills turned in the prairie breeze, where the car had just come from, and ahead, a tall water tower stood gleaming white in the rising sun.

Risking being caught by daylight, the traveler, feeling hungry, stopped at a restaurant on a street that grandly called itself Broadway, for something resembling breakfast. Choosing a secluded corner booth, the traveler ordered coffee, four eggs, and country sausage.

Protein seemed important at the moment.

The room was warm, noisy, and smelled of pancakes, maple syrup, and coffee. It was filled with a group of individuals who might have come straight from a Norman Rockwell painting—workmen, farmers, a woman who could easily have been the town's librarian, another who appeared to be a nurse—perhaps as many as twenty-five or thirty of them, mostly in late middle age, who swapped jokes and good-natured insults over their bacon, waffles, and French toast and were obviously long accustomed to having breakfast together every morning. It was going to be very dangerous to feed properly in a town as small as this one.

The same horrible music—"Stand By Your Man" this time—was being played in the kitchen, interspersed at intervals by the farm report.

"Lee-OH-tuh," said the waitress, as she delivered the stranger's food, correcting the traveler's pronunciation in response to a question about motels in the area. "I'm from Hayes, originally. I don't know why it's spelled the way it is. Must be some kind of Indian name."

"No, honey," said an elderly waitress who had overheard her younger colleague. "It was named after Leoti Kibbee, one of our local pioneers."

An elderly man in a plaid wool farmer's jacket swiveled on his stool at the breakfast bar. "I beg to disagree, Mabel," he said in a surprising Oxford accent. "The best evidence is that the town was named after lovely Leoti Gray, the daughter of one of its founding fathers."

"Never mind him," the younger waitress said, grinning at the old man. "What does he know? He's just a retired Kansas State history professor."

"And gentleman farmer, I'd have you add," he said.

"And gentleman farmer," the girl added.

The room filled with friendly laughter.

Although the building itself appeared to be Victorian, the walls of the restaurant had been paneled over with rough planks that must have weathered on the outside of a barn somewhere for at least a century. They were decorated, in turn, with butter churns, carpet beaters, pitchforks, hoes, and spades, patented apple corers and potato peelers, horse collars, and dozens of other, less recognizable objects.

One such object, iron, fist-sized, with a crank handle at one end, had a hand-lettered card tacked to the wall beside it: "Guess What It Is, Win A Free Steak Dinner For Two." The traveler knew what it was, but these people wouldn't want to know. A sort of sex-toy for the Inquisition, in the Middle Ages it had been known as "the pear of anguish."

How had it ended up in Kansas?

Between the arcane artifacts hung ancient-looking photographs framed under glass that told the story of a "Wichita County War" (oddly enough, the city of Wichita was at the opposite end of the state from the county of the same name) fought in 1887 with the town of Coronado, over which would become the county seat. It was described as "the bloodiest county seat fight in the history of the American west," implying that there had been other such conflicts. How very strange.

Figures so legendary that even the thoroughly European traveler recognized their names—Luke Short, Ed and Bat Masterson, Doc Holliday, Bill Tilghman, and three of the Earp brothers—had been involved.

It developed that the town had one motel, nearly next door to the restaurant. The traveler finished eating, paid a woman with blue hair at a cash register beside the door, and, pulling a hood up—it was a chilly morning, so it didn't look too strange—went out to face the dawn.

○

"I can't stop loving you! I've made up my mind..."

There was simply no getting away from the horrible music covering the prairie almost to the east coast. No wonder it was called the "Great American Desert." And what passed for music in the cities was worse.

The traveler snapped the clock radio off and hadn't even bothered with the television. Sleeping in silence was an old, rather pleasant habit in any case. In this tiny village there was so little traffic outside, it was almost like being back in the old country, in the old days.

Then, there had been no music at all. Remembering it as if it were yesterday, he fell asleep, and dreamed of it all through the daylight hours.

Arising as the sun set, blood screaming for blood, the traveler left the motel. The Firebird turned east toward an "historic" park a few blocks away which had been featured in a local tourist brochure that had been left in the room along with a Gideon Bible. The traveler cruised its edges until a sign of life was seen, a young man cleaning up around the fenceposts and the bases of trees with a powered leaf blower.

Nearby, the whitewashed bulk of a pair of cinderblock public rest-rooms could be seen, complete with glass brick windows and decorative scalloped cinderblock trim running around the rim of its roof.

Firebird parked neatly in one of the spaces marked off with yellow paint lines, the traveler headed toward the facility as if in urgent need of its amenities—an urgency did move the traveler now, but of a completely different order—passing by the outdoor janitor on the way.

"Bathroom's locked up, just now," the young man hollered after the hastening traveler. "I've got the keys. Let me come and unlock it for you."

The traveler nodded, having planned to call for help to attract the victim. Now it was unnecessary. Some people were so stupidly helpful. Waiting for the young man to unlock the door, when the lock finally clicked, the traveler seized him by the belt and pushed him inside, pulling the key from the lock and relocking the door from within.

"Hey! What'd you do that for?" the man complained, picking himself up from the floor. He took a fighting stance and balled his fists. The man was young, healthy, tall, well-muscled, and would have appeared daunt-ing to any other human being. To the traveler, he was simply food.

Without uttering a word, the traveler seized him, turned his head aside, bit deeply into his throat, relishing the steam arising in the un-heated room from the fresh blood that splashed to the floor between them. In a few moments, when the victim lay silent, motionless, and drained, the traveler washed up minimally in one of the sinks, exited the room and locked it again, throwing the man's keychain up onto the roof.

The Firebird turned west again, headed for the border, into night.

11: THE LOST PICCOLO

"All good is hard. All evil is easy. Dying, losing, cheating, and mediocrity is easy. Stay away from easy."—Scott Alexander

The whole thing started just before I went to see the dentist. I'd stopped off at a little restaurant across the street from the south side of the Ludwig von Mises Memorial College campus. The institution is very small—no more than fifteen hundred students in a given year—but its faculty and student body are very choosy when it comes to lunch.

Uncle Antoine's Basin Street Barbecue features an interesting combination of traditional Louisiana Cajun food, and Deep South barbecue. I'd never had anything from the menu that I'd disliked. Today I was here for the crustaceans: crawdads, crayfish, crawdaddies, whatever you want to want to call them. Uncle Antoine calls them "mudbugs."

Some of the best cuisine in the world has been nothing more than a result of destitute, hungry folks willing to try anything. I'm sure that was true of the first people who tried mudbugs. The traditional Cajun way is to boil them in a big cauldron with Andouille sausage, corn on the cob, quartered potatoes, and other stuff, plus a lot of seasonings that give the whole thing that French-Canadian-in-Exile flavor.

Mudbugs Evangeline *a la Oncle Antoine* was a much simpler dish, consisting of the eponymous arthropod steamed over beer—preferably Jax, once manufactured proudly on the river side of Jackson Square; Uncle Antoine claimed he had the last supply, but I suspected he was doing some decanting and recanting—served with drawn butter for the tail, cocktail sauce for the head, and French bread of course (hold the garlic, please), made right here in beautiful downtown New Prospect.

My plan was to buy a pound of grabbyfish, take them home, and share them with my loyal feline companion, as I usually did at this point in the week. Mudbugs taste a little bit like shrimp, a little bit like lobster (some obsessive-compulsives even crack and pick the meat out of their tiny claws) but with a subtle, beefy undertone all their own. The edibles inside the head, chock full of vitamins and stuff, remind me a little of the deviled egg yolks my mom used to make.

My plan, however, went bad when I was standing at the high, curved glass cabinet Uncle Antoine used for takeout. They'd just gotten my order (they'd probably started fixing it when they saw me getting out of the car) and the girl in a big white apron was serving a young woman and her little girl, eight or ten years old (I can't tell anymore, if I ever could) who wanted to know exactly what was in crawfish *etouffee.*

I was interested to hear about it, too, but I saw a reflection in the counter. Someone was at the little round table where the curious girl and her mommy had left their coats and purses, not six feet away. It was a kid—late teens or early twenties, pretorn jeans, ragged, dirty t-shirt, flip-flops, metal studs and rings inserted in his face everywhere you looked—rifling boldly and quickly through their bags.

"My piccolo!" yelled the outraged little girl, as the kid seized on a tiny zippered case that looked like it might have been made for a couple of stalks of celery (also good with mudbugs) and headed for the door.

I tossed one of my business cards at the mom and said, "Call me later!", then streaked across the little restaurant and slammed through the door. I didn't see the kid, at first, and the sun was shining too warmly for me to detect any lingering trace of body heat he might have left on the sidewalk. I couldn't smell him, either, maybe thanks to the Cajun spices. Most people will turn right without thinking when they're in a hurry and it doesn't matter. He looked like somebody who didn't do a lot of thinking, so that was the direction I headed.

Amazingly, it took me a whole three blocks to catch up with the piccolo thief. He was in an alley, crouching down behind a dumpster. More olfactory interference. But it was his pounding heartbeat—clearly audible to me and about a hundred to the minute—that gave him away. I stood over him. He tried to rise. I put a fastidious index finger atop his head (his long hair was greasy) and told him, "Stay put."

His hands were empty, and what he was wearing wouldn't have concealed what he'd taken, but I checked anyway, allowing him to pull his shirt up, turn out his pockets, and roll up his pants cuffs. I didn't want to touch him. I could tell that he was going to vomit any second.

"Calm down and tell me what you did with what you took."

"So you can use it as evidence to run me in?" He was surprisingly resistant.

I replied, "I'm not a cop. I have no intention of running you in. If I did, that little girl's piccolo would sit in evidence for weeks, not doing her any good. Tell me where you put it, and I will let you go."

"Yeah, right." I've run into people like that, who can resist my charms. I never met one who could keep it up forever—or much over ten minutes. In this guy's case, it was very likely drugs that were helping him. "If you're not a cop, show me that you're not carrying a badge."

"Sorry, I left the badge I don't have at home. But maybe this will help." One of the heavy metal lift straps on the dumpster had been dented inward, by collision with a wall or a truck or something. It was at least four inches wide and a quarter of an inch thick, ten or twelve inches of it, welded around the corner of the dumpster at both ends. I reached under it and without effort pulled it back into proper shape.

I bared my still untrimmed fangs. "Don't make me unhappy."

The thief gulped audibly. Then he pointed a shaky index finger at the dumpster. "It's in there," he squeaked. "You gonna let me go, now?"

"Not quite that easy. You threw it in there, you dig it out."

A couple of minutes later, he'd dug it out. It wasn't particularly difficult, being right on top of the trash. The climb I made him essay into the dumpster was meant more as punishment than practicality. The soft-sided plastic piccolo case cleaned up with no trouble. I had thought about making him lick it clean, but manfully restrained myself.

Mommy and daughter would be grossed out.

What I did do, once he climbed back out of the dumpster, was look him in the eye and push him just as hard as I could. "Don't do drugs any more, you don't need them. Clean yourself up. Get a job. Go back to school."

He assured me that he'd do all of those things. I was less than certain. The hardest thing in the world is for people to change their nature. Look at me, a vampire for the last 65 years, recovering a little girl's piccolo because I liked the questions she was asking at Antoine's.

While I was pocketing the piccolo, my telephone began playing R.E.M.'s "Losing My Religion." I flipped it open, saying, "This is J Gifford."

"Mr. Gifford, this is Alicia Kelvin—it's my daughter's piccolo that—"

"I've got it now and am heading back to Uncle Antoine's."

"You have it? Oh, dear—we're not there. We have an appointment with the orthodontist and had to leave. We're on our way there right now."

"Okay," I told her. "You can stop by my office any time and pick it up."
I gave her the address, which is not on the card. "By an odd coincidence,
I have a dentist's appointment, myself, in about fifteen minutes."

We agreed on a time, which is why I was back here at the house, waiting. They arrived right on the dot, and I let them in the front door.

"Here is your piccolo," I began, handing it to her. "I'm sorry, I don't
know your name. I know your mother's, because she told me on the phone."

The cat chose that moment to put in an appearance. Usually he won't
come in the office when I have clients. I suspected an ulterior motive.

"My name is Mary Frances Kelvin. Thank you for getting my piccolo.
I'm in the band at school. I don't know what I would have done without it."

"You're very welcome, Mary Frances Kelvin." Fiddlestring hopped up
into her lap, curled up, and made himself comfortable. I sat back in my
chair. "If I'm ever in need of a piccolo player, I'll know where to look."

Mary Frances giggled, and began stroking the cat. He began purring.

"What do we owe you?" the mom, Alicia, asked, getting out her check-
book. Judging by their shoes, they didn't have a lot to spare. There was
a story here—where was Mr. Kelvin, if there was a Mr. Kelvin?—but it
wasn't mine to pry into. Anyway, it didn't matter. I'd have done the same
thing for a rich kid if she'd been as smart and sweet.

"Absolutely nothing. It was my pleasure. The young fellow who took
it is very sorry now, and asks you to forgive him. He's a changed man." I
hoped he was a changed man. I knew he was sorry—for getting caught.

"You're sure?" I nodded. "Then we have something for you. We just
stopped by the restaurant and they're fresh and hot." Of course I knew
this was going to happen. I'd smelled what was in the shopping bag when
I let them in. But I pretended to be surprised and I really was pleased.

Rather than disturb the cat, Alicia rose and took the bag, which her
daughter had set down on the floor beside her chair. My kind of people.
"There's some French bread in there, and Uncle Antoine threw in an order
of ribs just to thank you for taking care of his other customers."

I opened the white plastic bag and looked inside. "Mudbugs!" I exclaimed. Fiddlestring and his boss were going to be happy campers
tonight.

I've always wondered what that means.

THE TRAVELER: COLORADO SPRINGS, COLORADO

"Stupidity is far more dangerous than evil, for evil takes a break from time to time, stupidity does not."—Anatole France

The traveler peeked out through heavy double curtains parted only a fraction of an inch, and winced at the sunlight harshly reflected from windshields and chromium on cars parked in front of the motel room.

It was unnervingly bright outside, and, according to the local weather report on television, the day was warm for this time of year. This was not the highest altitude the traveler had ever been to—Tibet beat it by a long way—but it was surprisingly difficult to breathe; some time must be allowed for adaptation. That was why the room had been paid for three days in advance. Rest and feed were the prescription.

Feed and rest.

It wasn't a particularly onerous task, even for one as energetic and restless as the traveler usually was. There was a specialized television channel that featured numerous documentaries about the ancient homeland—the traveler was coming to love these Americans and even their whiny, pathetic hangers-on the British—speculating in a hundred different ways on what must have happened back in those times to account for the way that things had turned out in the world today.

All that they had to guess by were bones and stones.

The whole thing was very gratifying, even if the "scientists" had most of the facts wrong. In this, considered as reporters, they were little different from that portion of the news media who were focused on the present. It was somehow personal, like getting notices the day after your performance in a play. The traveler had changed the course of human history

66

from time to time in ways that they would never know. Or be willing to accept. Yet it had never been by any intention but necessity.

The traveler thought about youthful times for a while. Memories of them were as sharp and clear as the memories of yesterday. The snow, the glaciers, the loess, the animals. There was a zoo in this city, according to various pamphlets in the room, that might have been worth visiting, if only to see animals reminiscent of days long past. It was impossible, of course, forbidden by evolution and the ungentle facts of unfriendly reality. The sun was Enemy, a hateful, baleful, lethal, featureless face in the sky that frowned on those who dared to live forever.

But it would have been nice to see an elephant and imagine it with hair.

It was still too early to be out and about, but the traveler had noticed an abandoned mall across the interstate highway from this motel. Another monument to the eternal greed, stupidity, and perfidy of princes, its exterior windows covered with plywood, the plywood covered with graffiti. He decided to explore it after dark. There might be an artist or two to catch there and teach the error of their ways.

The traveler would enjoy that, very much.

Just now, it was better to rest in the cool, dark refuge of this rented room, and even better yet to take the victims of the next few nights' explorations somewhere that the spilling of blood wouldn't matter. Somewhere that no one would hear them scream with surprise and pain.

The traveler looked forward to it with an appetite that never waned. But for now, the thing to do was rest and await the coming darkness.

Laugh at the humans' silly guesses.

And dream of home and times long past.

○

Moving with the shadows in the failing daylight, the traveler drifted across the highway toward the abandoned mall. There was prey to be had here beyond a doubt. They could be smelled a hundred meters away: male and female, young and vital, with just the faintest hint of illegal drugs of various kinds coursing through arteries inflamed by testosterone, in the case of the males, and by fear in the case of the females.

To the traveler, it was like a feast of spicy delicacies laid out on a groaning table, to be anticipated by the one about to partake of it and savored like Mexican green chili, a good Indian curry, or kung pao.

In one place, toward the rear of the mall, away from the road and the prying eyes of local police and the highway patrol, one of the sheets of graffiti-covered plywood had been loosened so that it hung by one corner and could be swung up and away to the passage of human beings.

And their motorcycles.

Inside, as it grew darker now by the minute, the traveler could smell a small fire, fed by scraps and debris that littered the place and watch its flickering, dancing glow reflected along the building's inner walls. Vapors released from various plastics and the dried paint on the burning junk would undoubtedly shorten the lives of the fire-builders faster and more certainly than any drugs they might be using.

Drugs, poisons, and diseases in the blood of victims had never represented a problem to the traveler. Some variety of magic—or perhaps it was simply the unromantic but more scientific fact that traveler and prey were of different species—had always seemed to neutralize whatever potential threat presented itself. The Black Death, the ergot-inspired mass insanity of the Dark Ages, the waves of New World venereal disease that had swept the Old World during the Age of Discovery, the so-called Spanish Influenza, the AIDS phenomenon, none of them had meant anything at all to the traveler except easier prey.

The traveler suspected that the local authorities knew perfectly well that the property was being used this way. Better to keep these miscreants where one knew where they were, than drive them away into places where they might possibly disturb or frighten taxpayers and voters.

"Whatcha doin' in here, slow-ped?"

The young specimen suddenly confronting the traveler was short but broad, covered with tattoos that were too new to be faded but too old to be garish. He was pierced in at least a dozen places and had shaved his head, saving only a small scalp-lock at the back, bound up in a colored cord. He was bare to the waist, except for a black leather vest that matched his trousers and bore various arcane markings, including the name and symbol of his affiliate tribal grouping, "The Reptiles."

In one hand he held another of those "knuckle duster" knives that seemed so popular in America, this one with a long, sharp, curving blade.

Over the ages, the traveler had found scant use for weapons and never carried any. Tearing one's enemies and prey apart with one's naked hands and bared fangs worked as well, and was infinitely more satisfying.

At need, the traveler could quell a distant foe with casual ease, depending on superior strength and superhuman eye-hand coordination to throw a stone the size of two fists, for example, a hundred meters or more and invariably strike with deadly accuracy. No jumped-up king's thug, no matter how well armored and mounted, had ever bested the traveler.

And, of course, on the rare occasion that the traveler felt a weapon was needed, it could always be taken from an enemy within arm's reach.

"You're my first," gloated the tattooed youth, amateurishly rotating the tip of his knife in tiny circles. "This is gonna set me up!"

Wordless, the traveler reached out with a hand vastly swifter than the quickest viper and seized the young man's extended knife hand, pulling it to the right so the youth wound up with his back to the predator.

"Hey, that's not—!"

Reaching over the young man's left shoulder, the traveler hooked fingers under the right side of his jaw, canted it, exposing his neck, and sank long fangs into flesh. Whatever fresh, hot blood the traveler didn't take coursed freely down the front of the young man's body. He managed another, rather pathetic scream—more of a whimper, really, thought the traveler, who was an expert in such matters—and fell limp. Not wanting to spoil the rest of the evening—the traveler had plans for the others of the gang—he was permitted to fall where he stood.

"What the fuck?" That from another figure, similarly attired, but older, his hair and beard beginning to show traces of gray. Standing in the sagging remains of a doorway, in one tattooed hand he held a long screwdriver, from the other swung the greasy drive chain of a motorcycle.

"He's done Ratty!" observed another tribesman, from behind the first. Behind him, other figures had begun to pile up, the rearmost of them "old ladies"—the women, slaves and volunteers alike, of the tribe.

"Holy shit!" several of them exclaimed at once.

The traveler lifted one hand, palm up, and beckoned with crooked fingers. It was a gesture from one of the rare motion pictures that the vampire had seen—at a Budapest theater full of warm, delicious schoolgirls, crowded shoulder to shoulder, if memory served—and liked.

This will be fun.

12: DINNER IN A DUNGEON

"Good can imagine Evil; but Evil cannot imagine Good."—W. H. Auden

Next afternoon, when I finally woke up—Fiddlestring and I had enjoyed mudbugs and old movies into the early hours—I got up, drank some blood from the refrigerator (I should do something about feeding fresh as soon as possible, I reminded myself), ate a quick breakfast, fed the cat, whose belly was so round and taut he didn't really care, and drove to the hospital, a little worried about what I might find there.

I needn't have worried, as it turned out. When I elevatored to the oncology floor, Priscilla was sitting up, surrounded by her adoring family. With her were Anton, their son Patrick, and their daughter Amber. Priscilla's color had come back, and she looked ten years younger already.

"J!" she exclaimed when she saw me standing in the door. I'd stopped off at a florist and bought her a big bouquet of black-eyed susans, their stems cradled in the fat arms of a small plaid teddy bear.

Yeah, I know.

Amber, a lithe and willowy strawberry blond, flowed from the corner she had occupied of her mother's bed, stood on tiptoe to give me a big kiss on the cheek despite the sun block—like her brother, the girl had grown up thinking she knew what was wrong with me—then stood beside me with her arms around my neck, and turned toward her mother.

From the day she was born, she'd always been able to make me smile no matter how generally rotten things were, otherwise. I gave her a hug. But not too big. She was a grown woman now, and my surrogate daughter.

"Hiya, Mrs. V.," I said over the top of Amber's head. "You look great! Have any fresh air and sunshine yet?" Of course I had a reason—an extremely important reason—for asking her about that. By now, Patrick, in civilian clothing, had arisen from the Comfy Chair and I disdained his proffered handshake, giving him a great big hug, too, instead.

I sent the kids back to their mom, taking a couple of steps closer to the bed, myself. I nodded at Anton. He nodded back, abstractedly. The man seemed oblivious to everything but the fact, I surmised, that his Priscilla wasn't going to die any time soon. As far as I was concerned, Anton could be as abstracted as he wanted. I didn't blame him.

She grinned. "As a matter of fact, we just came in from the roof. Plenty of sunshine, but not very much fresh air. All we could smell was that little Vietnamese restaurant across the street, serving lunch." She closed her eyes, remembering. "Actually, it smelled pretty good."

I laughed. "I noticed it when I got here. Hot and sour soup—my favorite." Basically, food is my favorite dish. "Add a big handful of crispy noodles, you've got the breakfast of champions. So tell me what makes you so bright and chirpy this fine afternoon? Last time I saw you—"

"Don't remind me, please!" She grimaced. It was like the lights in the room had dimmed. "I can barely remember seeing you. It's like a dream."

"More like a nightmare, if I was in it." The lights came back up again.

Anton spoke. "Nobody understands it. Two days ago, they said—you know what they said—but now it's all but gone. 'Spontaneous remission,' as if naming it explains it. A fucking miracle, I call it!"

Patrick made a sour face. "Now don't get religion on us, Dad. The human body is a marvelous thing, and Mom is a pretty determined critter—"

"I am *not* a critter, Patrick Aloysius Varick!" The boy's real name was John Patrick, and Priscilla was laughing as she said it. I was so relieved I thought my knees were going to give out on me. She wasn't going to die and she wasn't going to be a vampire. Two out of two. I made a mental note to get ahold of her charts and test results, somehow, to make damned sure that she wouldn't be requiring a second "treatment."

I bent down to give her a peck on the cheek, stood up, and said, "Sorry to run. I have work to do this afternoon. Should I come back tonight?"

They all agreed I should. I excused myself, walked out of the room considerably lighter of heart, took the elevator down to the ground floor and the covered walkway to the tree-shaded part of the parking lot. Around the hospital and across the street, I parked again and entered Saigon Gone. A big bowl of soup and an order of Vietnamese eggrolls later, I pointed the Suburban's blunt nose east and headed home.

O

There was mail in the box when I got back. After I garaged the car, I went through the house to the front, collected it, and took it to my desk. The usual, for the most part: bills, insurance ads, fliers from the hardware store, something from the AARP—if they only knew. On the other hand, they could probably teach me a thing or three about bloodsucking.

Fiddlestring joined me, taking the chair across the desk from me, as if he were a brand new client. He meowed a greeting at me. I meowed back.

"What do we have here?" I asked him rhetorically. There was also a fat Number 10 envelope with my name neatly hand-printed on it, but no address or stamp. I held it up to the light, which was kind of stupid, gave it a sniff—strong lilac scent, like a sachet in a little old lady's underwear drawer—then found my letter opener, an authentic sliver of the decking of the H.M.S. *Victory*—and slit the top across.

"Holy shit!"

Whoever it was, they sure as hell knew how to impress a guy. Inside I discovered no fewer than two dozen twenty dollar bills—twenty-five, as it turned out, five hundred bucks even—and a note, written in the same ballpoint as the envelope, but in a nicely rounded cursive that looked feminine, and a bit foreign, for some reason. The lilac scent came from a cardboard air freshener, like you find at a filling station or automotive parts store and hang from your rear view mirror.

"Please accept this money as a retainer or down payment. I have information for you and employment. Meet me at eight o'clock at Boiling Oil, downstairs. The reservation will be in the name of Sava Savanovic."

I'd heard that name before, somewhere.

"What's a Sava Savanovic?" I asked Fiddlestring, but the big orange bum didn't answer. I hadn't forgotten the phony *federale* that Quinn, Quyen, and T.W. had warned me was sniffing around lately, but if this was his work, it was probably best just to confront him and get it over with quick. Besides, one person's blood is as good as any other's.

Boiling Oil was a fondue place between the college and downtown New Prospect, in a former industrial area undergoing gentrification. It was new and I hadn't eaten there yet, but I'd meant to for some time. Somebody had taken an old brick factory building, erected a crenellated top along the facade, and added arched doors and a pair of cylindrical brick towers at the front corners, with conical slate roofs. All they were missing was a moat, drawbridge, and portcullis. What had once been a basement was now "Ye Dungeon," the chicest bar in town.

Sava Savanovic. It was six o'clock already. I tucked the money back into the envelope, and the envelope into the office safe. I would take it to the restaurant in case I had to turn the job down. I called Anton to let him know I wouldn't be showing up tonight after all, then went upstairs to shower and change my clothes, not necessarily in that order.

Fiddlestring followed me until I got into the shower.

The big sissy.

○

Boiling Oil didn't require me to wear a necktie, but settled for my open-collared shirt, Duluth Trading Company "firehose" sports jacket with about half a billion pockets, and navy blue Dockers. Among other things, the jacket concealed my old Bianchi 9R shoulder holster in which the .38 Detective Special was slung upside-down under my left armpit.

Six rounds of Glaser Safety Slugs made up for the weakness of .38 Special. Twelve more in Safariland speedstrips added to the comfort factor.

I told the pretty girl standing at the podium near the entrance "Sava Savanovic," resisting the urge to whisper, and feeling like what I'd really said was "swordfish." Another cute young thing grabbed a couple of giant menus and led me on the most amazing and circuitous trek through the restaurant, which had begun its life long ago as a burlap bag factory, down a flight of stairs, across that floor, filled with happy, chattering customers playing with small cauldrons of heated liquids, down another flight of stairs, and to a little corner booth, surrounded on two sides by glassed-in wine racks full of tilted bottles.

She lifted a four-inch circular cover in the middle of the table, exposing a small gas burner, lit the flame, took my drink order—Cuervo 1800 and a glass of lemonade—and left. I looked around. It was dark, sort of cozy, in a way that reminded one of medieval torture chambers. Other customers, mostly couples, were cooking things in oil, cheese, or a mix of kirsch and chocolate. The aromas were absolutely wonderful. Not for the first time, I wondered who I'd be enjoying them with.

I waited fifteen minutes, twenty minutes, twenty-five, growing edgier by the nanosecond. My drink came and I did it some serious damage.

And then...

I could smell her before I saw her, but it was still a life shattering surprise when she came around the corner, through the door, and sat down across from me. My heart was pounding so hard that it hurt inside my chest, and I could hear hers pounding just as hard, as well.

She smiled, pointing to the wine racks that surrounded us.

"Just like old times, isn't it, my love?"

13: PRISONER OF HISTORY

"Neither gods nor men can foresee when an evil deed
will bear its fruit."—Bodhidharma

Surica.

I had probably imagined this moment maybe a million times in the sixty-five years since I'd last seen her. That's only forty-two times a day, or about twice per waking hour. Like I said, I don't sleep much.

Surica.

Now just the sight of her, the scent of her, the sound of her voice had me paralyzed. All the things I ever thought I'd say if this day ever came were absent from my mind, leaving nothing behind but vacuum.

Surica.

"You don't know how flattered I am that you've remembered me," she said. She could hear my heart beating just as easily as I could hear hers. Neither of us was doing this particularly well, but she was ahead of me by two whole sentences, one of them with a subordinate clause.

"How could I ever forget the girl who gave me eternal life?" There was more I wanted to say, a lot more. But the waiter arrived to take our order. He would look at her, then look away, blushing, then look again. He stammered and made mistakes, so I knew two things. First, the guy wasn't gay. Second, I wasn't the only one she had that effect on.

Surica had chosen the basic "little black dress" of song and legend, cut low enough to show about a mile of cleavage, high enough to display her remarkable legs. The dress was shimmery, composed of big sequins or something like that, put together in horizontal rows like ancient scale armor. They moved with her, and showed off every contour of her lush, supple body. Her stockings were fairly dark, worn with four-inch black pumps, and instead of the traditional string of pearls, she wore faceted hematite, with small, simple ear baubles to match.

We ate, choosing tidbits from a stainless steel plate—beef, pork, chicken, shrimp, lobster—impaling them on a long, slender fork, plunging them into a pot of boiling oil the waiter had placed over the burner. Before that, it had been bits of bread in melted cheese.

"Of course it is not lamb haggis," Surica laughed, "but then, what is?"

She chose a *pinot noir* and I stuck with tequila. I hardly tasted anything I ate. I was too busy convincing myself the woman—she still looked 17—seated across the table from me was real. I could see her. I could hear her. I could smell her. But could I believe that she was really here—I might be lying in the street right now with my head crushed by a truck—and that what she had to tell me was the truth?

She put a hand on mine. We hadn't touched each other before now. For my part, I didn't dare, we'd never be able to come back to this restaurant. Her finger along the back of my hand felt like an electric shock.

"I know you have many questions, my love. I have questions of my own to ask. Shall we wait until later this evening, perhaps another place, to begin answering one another, or would you rather start right now?"

"Let's start now. If we wait, we'll be too busy to answer questions."

She laughed, and I knew that she was still mine. Or mine again. "I have much to tell you, my love, much I hope you will believe. You can hear my heartbeat as I hear yours. I share your olfactory powers, so you will know if I lie to you. I only mention it because, where I have come from, everybody lies about everything and expects you to lie, as well."

"I'll believe you," I told her, and I meant it. "Just tell me why you left, Surica, why it took 65 years to come back to me." It felt like opening my veins and letting six decades of pain flow out on the table.

She took a deep breath and exhaled. "I don't know why I left you there, in that village, the way I did. For all that I was 233 years old, I believe that I had never been in love before. It frightened me to have become so dependent, so quickly, upon the feelings of another person."

She looked at me to see if I could understand and accept that. I nodded, and turned my hand over, taking her hand into mine and squeezing.

"I followed the German soldiers out of the village," she went on, "feeding on unlucky stragglers, until I broke off to find my little airplane. She was sitting on her nose as I had left her, her propeller crumpled, her back broken, leaning against a couple of big trees, a total loss, just as I had remembered. I took a few things, an electric torch, a compass, a survival knife, a big toolbar, and then I set her afire.

"By then I had had some time to think, and it was my intention to return to you. But a series of unforeseen events occurred, preventing it. My squadron members, all female, had seen me go down, of course, and because their missions frequently carried them over the crash site, never gave up looking for me. They saw the fire. The British Army, warned that I suffered a disease that limited me to night missions—"

"Were they vampires, too? Your squadron members?" I was reminded that I'd never yet encountered another vampire, except for lovely Surica.

"No, just Romanians and unusually understanding. The British found me in the forest and returned me to my unit. When the Nazi government in Romania collapsed, we all went home—only to be swept up by the Soviets."

By then, I was halfway home, myself, in the hold of a Lithuanian freighter.

Surica continued. "I was sent to a 'special' prison, an ancient stone fortress high in the southwestern Carpathian Mountains, but deep down in a chasm where the direct rays of the sun reached perhaps only two hours a day in what passed there for summer. In addition, the region was densely wooded with dark evergreens, the old fortress lost in a kind of perpetual twilight. They were keeping other prisoners there, but they held me and a dozen others in the lowest dungeon of the place, and let us up and out to exercise for perhaps an hour each week."

The waiter came by to see if we needed anything. I ordered some of that chocolate stuff and another round of Cuervo and lemonade. Surica claimed she didn't want dessert, as women will, but had more wine.

"It was cold in that place, my love," she said, unconsciously holding her hands over the burner and rubbing them together. "So cold that the surface of the water in the trough they gave us froze and had to be broken every morning. So cold that I could feel my heart and pulse slow. But that was certainly not going to kill me. There was very little food, and the water I mentioned was not good, but I could survive no matter what lived in it, and there were small animals—but you don't want to hear of that. I don't like thinking of it, even now."

I chuckled, having eaten rats in that ship I'd stowed away on, and nearly went into some kind of suspended animation myself, thanks to the cold. The only bright spot—if you want to call it that—was that a crewman would show up every day, on inspection rounds, so I didn't lack for fresh blood. But I kept my mouth shut, not wanting to interrupt.

"The others on that level, who shared a large cell with me, were not vampires. I believe that my captors expected me to feed on them, and perhaps even communicate what I was to them. Because I had no other choice, I took a little blood, a few milliliters at a time, and did not infect them, not at first. They died, one by one—no, I did not kill them, it was the cold, starvation, and filth—but in the end, I tried to help them, giving them small amounts of my own blood. In the end, they all died anyway, leaving only me to suffer, all alone. And in many ways, that was far worse than any other kind of privation.

"I believe that the Communists knew what I was all along and were preserving me to see if I might be 'weaponized' in some way. After my cellmates were gone, a failed experiment, if I was correct, a number of 'volunteers' were sent to feed me, children of local farmers, mostly, a different individual every day. I received a little news that way, although I chose not to believe most of it. Assassinated leaders I could accept, but people walking on the Moon? I gave a bit of myself to my 'victims,' leaving them with happy, if totally false memories.

"Finally, as the guards grew increasingly lax and slovenly—I didn't know for certain that the government was collapsing, but I had begun suspecting it—I was able to escape when they brought me a new 'victim.'

"Overpowering the single dungeon guard, I quickly took the stairs and killed the second in command of the place, drinking him as dry as I could before I snapped his neck. His office safe yielded to me in a matter of seconds—you could hear the ancient tumblers fall all the way across the room. Inside I discovered a lot of useless paper money, watches, rings, and other jewelry they'd stolen from their unfortunate prisoners.

"There was a bit of gold in small, crudely-cast bars. I hated to think where it might have come from; these Communist thugs were every bit as bad as the Nazis had been. But I took it anyway, as I would need it. And—I couldn't believe it after all these years—my own personal service pistol, well greased and still in its flapped military holster, complete with its spare magazine. The new regime, I learned later, used an entirely different issue sidearm and cartridge, but in this badly neglected backwater, the old ammunition was still issued.

"There were half a dozen boxes in the safe.

"Fearing what they had heard of me, I suppose, the rest of the prison staff, no more than a dozen, had fled. I was aware that the officer I'd killed was only filling in for the commander, and reasoned that his superior—the Warden—had departed, as well. I took what warm winter clothing and other things I wanted—food was important; I knew I wouldn't need credentials—opened up all of the cell doors to let my fellow prisoners out, and then urged them to scatter in all directions.

"Many of them wouldn't go, but huddled in their cells, afraid.

"But following my own advice, I headed southwest, to the nearest airfield, or, failing that, the Black Sea. I soon learned that there had been a revolution against the Communist regime, and the year was 1989.

"I had been a captive for 45 years."

14: DARKNESS AND DEATH

"Destroy the seed of evil, or it will grow up to your ruin."—Aesop

*V*isibly trying to shake off the memory of her ordeal, Surica said, "Now you will take me home—I have seen your home, of course; it is very nice—make love to me, and I will tell you of a problem that I have."

"A problem that you have?" I repeated, not too bright.

"Not now," she breathed. "Afterward."

She paid the bill in cash and I let her. We got up from the little table. She held out a shawl or light scarf that I hadn't noticed before. It was black and sheer and sparkly. She turned and I draped it across her smooth, white shoulders. Then she picked up a handbag that matched the whole outfit, and we found our way across the restaurant and upstairs—it was practically a religious experience, watching her negotiate the steps in those heels—and out into the parking lot.

I'd brought the Cruiser. Surica had come in a cab, she told me.

At a spot on the sidewalk where the shadow of a tree provided us a little privacy from the streetlight, she turned to me, threw her arms around

my neck and kissed me passionately and deeply. I returned the kiss, seizing her around her slender waist. For a while we were lost in time and
space, both of us remembering what had happened between us sixty-five
years ago, both of us anticipating what was going to happen now.

At last we broke for air like a couple of teenagers, still hungry for each
other. Surica smiled and patted my coat on the left-hand side, under my
arm. "J Gifford, Private Eye. Only you weren't J Gifford back in France,
were you? Is that your *roscoe* or are you just glad to see me?"

"If I'm showing it there, we've got a problem. Yes, I'm glad to see you,
but that is my roscoe. Also my gat, my heater, my piece, and my strap.
What've you got, weighing down the corner of your bag like that?"

She grinned. "My old service pistol. It suits me and I'm used to it." She
stopped and looked around. It was later than I realized and the parking
lot was nearly empty. "Is that your car? It's really cute!"

"Just what every macho American male wants to hear—his car is cute."
As I was letting her into the passenger side, like a gentleman, she whispered something in my ear that every macho American male would give
several semi-important body parts to hear, and then nibbled my earlobe.

Once we were in the car, I turned and pulled her to me as much as
the damned unromantic bucket seats would permit. I kissed her for a
long, long time, touched her face—there were tears streaming down her
cheeks—and I explored again the first part of her that I'd ever touched.
Full and firm. I reached beneath the top of her dress and discovered that
she wasn't wearing a bra. She closed her eyes and moaned into my mouth
as I rolled her nipple between my thumb and forefinger.

Whatever it was we'd had in that wine cellar in France, apparently we
still had it. I was either in heaven—or a hell of a lot of trouble.

Either way, it was going to be a very long drive home.

○

If I were to describe exactly what happened between Surica and me
over the next several hours, this would be a very different kind of story—
one much better suited to some of the shadier reaches of the Internet. Or
the kind of bookstores they set up in abandoned gas stations.

From the first moment we had met, back in that French wine cellar, there had been no barriers between us, nothing held back, nothing
denied. It was no different now, sixty-five years later. Whatever it was
that filled me with energy and passion at the faintest touch of her skin,
the least smell of her fragrance, the least sound of her voice, and the

least sight of her face and body, it had not faded over the better part of a century. In fact it seemed stronger than ever before.

I had never understood what it was that Surica saw (or felt or heard or smelled) in me. It was a miracle that this small town boy from rural Illinois didn't want to question or inspect out of fear of destroying it, like a particularly beautiful and fragile soap bubble. As far as I could tell (and I can tell a lot farther than the average individual), she was as happy as I was and that was all I needed to know.

There are only so many things that two individuals can do with one another, and we did each and every one of them, and then did them all again. We would have bought the t-shirt if there had been one. Being a vampire means never having to say you're not quite ready yet, dear. The flesh has many fewer limits, and the mind and heart, no limits at all.

O

At some point, one of us said, "Think we'd better find somewhere to feed?" It wasn't clear which one of us it was until Surica answered me.

"Where do you usually go?" She propped her head up on one of her hands, resting on her elbow. The result was extremely scenic. There had been a little minor erotic bloodletting—vampires do that, you know—the sheets were a mess. I'd be buying a lot of bleach from now on.

"Meaning, who do I usually bite? Or is that 'whom'?" I wasn't ready to introduce Surica yet to Anton and his family—I wondered how Priscilla was doing—and that was the last way I wanted to do it. But what I said was, "I guess I forgot to tell you that I don't bite."

Wincing, she rubbed a couple of places on her throat and breasts. "I thought that you were biting pretty well a little while ago, Mr. Gifford."

"That's different." I described the process, Vacutainers, hypos, including giving the victim back a little of my blood. When I'd first arrived in New Prospect, I'd looked for winos, alley lurkers, bag ladies, and other such people, but it was always so depressing, and without passing any judgment, I always felt I was extending a life of misery.

She considered it for a moment. "That's very clever, J. And much neater. I wish that I'd thought of it. So where should we go for 'breakfast'?"

I confessed that I didn't have a good idea, explaining about my friends, and that I wanted her to meet them in a different context, first.

"When I'm in a strange town," she suggested, "I always go the library."

I lifted a heavy strand of her deep auburn hair from her face, where it crossed one lovely brown eye and put it back in place. "The library?"

"For the most part," she nodded, flopping the strand back across her face, "the people you meet there are clean and relatively free of diseases."

"You're pretty clever, yourself, Miss Fieraru. Do you do it in the stacks?"

"My love, you know I'll do it with you anywhere—oh, you mean feeding. No, I wait until somebody goes to the bathroom and I follow her in. Normally it's women. Men, if the thirst is on me. It's over in a moment."

I blinked. "You don't mean you—"

"Kill them? Absolutely not, my darling. They feed me and then they forget, just as yours do. Most probably I don't take any more blood for sustenance than you do. It's unnecessary to kill people. They don't deserve that. And leaving a trail of dead bodies for no good reason is what got most vampires hunted down and killed in centuries past."

"Centuries past. Surica, have you ever met another vampire?"

"To speak to? Only one. He's the problem I need to talk to you about..."

"The one who sired you?" I admit I'd taken the expression from TV.

"I don't know who sired me, J. I don't understand how the biology works. Perhaps you do. It is entirely possible there was more than one."

"More than one sire—but how—"

"Be patient, my love, and I will tell you. The year, as you know, was 1728. I was on the way to an arranged marriage in Serbia, to a very rich, very fat, very old man. I was but a girl of seventeen, and it was a marriage of which I wanted no part. Nevertheless, both of my parents insisted, as it would end certain financial difficulties they were having, and it would enhance the family's prestige in our part of Romania."

"Nice folks."

"They were people of their times, no more, no less. Their only asset, their daughter, at seventeen was threatening to become an old maid. Besides, they told me, my fiance, whom I had never met, was old and might not impose upon me too much. And besides that, he might die soon."

"Like I said, nice folks."

"Our traveling party, consisting of two coaches, two drivers and two footmen, two ladies' maids and four heavily armed outriders, was compelled to stop in the darkest heart of the forest one night because there was no hospitality within easy traveling time. Once we had settled in, we were attacked without warning by bandits—vampire bandits."

I didn't know what to say, and so I nodded. She went on.

"Our male servants, all of our outriders, drivers, and footmen, discharged their various weapons at the bandits, utterly to no avail. The same was true, as well, of my father, with his brace of little silver Scottish pistols. They were all killed immediately, in that unnecessary, ugly manner I abhor, as the women were compelled to watch."

I put a hand on hers. Her tear-rimmed eyes were full of horror.

"They took their time with the women, by turns raping and feeding upon them, abusing them in other ways, passing them back and forth among themselves. Having seen my father brutally killed, now I watched my mother die, as well, savaged for the amusement of the animals using her, unable to bear the humiliation of it and live. I recall it only in flashes, bits and pieces, as I was being used exactly the same way, myself.

"One girl, my mother's maid, had particularly large breasts. They bit into her nipples as she screamed, and suckled her blood, fed from her like babies, as a kind of terrible joke, until daylight finally forced them back into the black depths of the forest whence they had come.

"They killed the poor girl and left her lying, discarded, where they had repeatedly used her. I was supposed to have been killed, too. They certainly left me for dead, drained and defiled, face down like a broken doll in a deep pile of moldy leaves at the base of an ancient tree.

"I awoke to find that the sunlight was hurting me and, being a Romanian, I knew precisely what that meant. The coaches had been destroyed, smashed apart, used by the bandits to fuel their festive bonfire. Salvaging what I could of our scattered belongings, I covered my nakedness and made my way, by night, along the road to my fiance's estate—we had been more than halfway there when we were attacked—until I ran into a company of men, sent to discover why we had not yet arrived.

"By then, my outward wounds had already begun healing. My inner wounds would require more time. Having told the men what befell us— leaving out only the part about vampires—I traveled back with them to tell their master the same story. Give him his due, he married me, just as he had sworn he would, but he never touched me, never made a single demand upon me of any kind. It could simply be that he was old and incapable. Or it could be that, having been gang-raped in that vile forest, I was now in some way unclean, tainted by the evil that everywhere had penetrated my body and spent itself inside me. It was just as well, however. It was years—decades, actually—before I could begin to contemplate being intimate with anyone, under any circumstances.

"The old man died before the year was out. He had found ways, in a benighted day and age where women were not permitted to inherit or own property, to leave everything that he possessed to me. Once assured of this legacy, I assembled a group of soldiers—mercenaries—and, equipped with sword, *main gauche*, and a pair of long, large-caliber, double-barreled flintlock pistols, in all of which I had spent the whole year training, rode at their head back toward that dark forest road.

"Each of us carried only ammunition cast laboriously from pure silver. Our edged weapons, too, were chased in the metal that kills vampires.

"Presenting ourselves to the eyes and ears of the wood as harmless travelers, we built our camp one night and waited. When the vampires came, we sprang our trap, and when we were through, there were thirty man-sized heaps of ash upon the ground, and half of my mercenaries lay dead, as well. Raking through the piles of ash—the mercenaries refused to do it—I discovered bits of jewelry and other personal effects that had once belonged to my mother and father, or to their servants.

"At last they—and their daughter, as well—had been revenged.

"We buried our fallen and departed."

15: *DEABRU*

"In battling evil, excess is good; for he who is moderate in announcing the truth is presenting half-truth."—Kahlil Gibran

*W*e paid a visit to the library downtown as soon as it opened the next morning. Fortunately, it was an unusually rainy day, so heavily overcast that it almost seemed like night, and we could leave our hats and coats and sunblock—Surica used the stuff, too—locked in the Suburban.

When the moment of truth arrived, I found that I couldn't just accost some other guy in a public bathroom. Too much of the middle class midwestern male left in me, I suppose. I was happy to "make do" with one of the assistant librarians in a closet marked "Staff Only." I drew enough blood, two Vacutainers' worth, for a couple of days, and the young lady went back to her work, relaxed and clear-headed, the cold symptoms that she'd been exhibiting already starting to diminish.

She showed me how to erase the surveillance tapes, which I did.

I met Surica in the fiction section, as we'd previously arranged, somewhere between Colin Wilson and F. Paul Wilson. She'd had a close encounter of the thirst kind with a young female Chinese student. I suppressed a smart-ass remark about Asian food. We went back to the house for real breakfast—after an appetizer consisting of each other.

"I like this business with the needles," she told me as I was flipping six eggs over medium. "It is tidier and more...humane, somehow. And returning just a bit, I do not feel so much like a monster."

She was sitting on a barstool at the counter in my kitchen, playing with Fiddlestring who had hopped right up there just as if it wasn't one of the five or six things he was absolutely not allowed to do. He lay on his side, purring, batting at her hand as she touched him quickly on each paw, at random, and on his nose and the tip of his tail.

I turned to grin at her. "Oh, you're still a monster, sweetheart. So am I. You're just a monster who pays her own way." But suddenly, she came around the counter and her mouth was on me again, and mine on her, our clothes scattering, and we were pretty much silent for a while, absurdly there on the kitchen floor. The cat had made himself scarce.

Around ten, finishing up my eggs—I'd burnt the first batch—and hashbrowns, I called Anton's cell phone number, but I got Amber, instead.

"We're going home!" she told me. "Dad's in there helping mom pack up. They can't find any trace of cancer in her, and they're chasing each other around in circles about it. They all wanted to do about seventy-five more tests on her, but Dad said no, it's time to go home."

Naturally, I was absolutely elated. Surica saw the look on my face and raised her pretty eyebrows. The dear girl hadn't gotten entirely dressed again and was a considerable distraction. I hadn't told her anything yet about what I'd done for (or to) Priscilla. I exchanged a few more happy words with Anton's daughter, broke the connection, and was about to fill Surica in, figuratively speaking, when the damn phone rang in my hand. I hate it when that happens. It always makes me jump.

"J Gifford. How may I help you?"

"Oh, I don't know," replied a familiar voice in a thick New Jersey accent. "I've been told I'm pretty much beyond help." I could hear a little silver laughter tinkling in the background, coming from Quyen. "I think we need to talk to you, J. Some pretty odd things have been happening."

"Okay," I told Quinn. "Does it have to do with that fake fed asking about me that you told me about?" I'd said it that way so Surica could follow me. "My dentist has apparently had a similar experience."

"Can we just come over and talk?" Quinn asked, clearly disturbed.

"Sure you can. Anyway, I have someone special to introduce you to."

I heard a hand go over the mouthpiece of the phone at the other end of the line. "He got laid, Quyen! Gifford finally got himself laid!"

I realized suddenly that Surica could hear Quinn on the phone as clearly as I could. I turned to her, blushing, and she was laughing at me.

I hung up and said, "Now while we have time, tell me about your problem."

○

Surica picked up her clothes from the floor and started putting them on. It made me sad to see her do that. To be absolutely fair, I'd gotten dressed. Popping grease is harmful to gonads and other living things.

As she dressed, she spoke, her accent growing thicker as memory flooded her mind. "Remember that I told you that the Warden of that prison in Romania where I spent a lifetime had fled by the time I escaped."

"Yes, I remember that." I put stuff in the dishwasher and started it. Ingredients went away, into cabinets and my enormous double-sided refrigerator. My kitchen was absolutely spotless and I could cook, too.

Someday I was going to make somebody a wonderful wife.

"I never understood," she told me, "while I was in that prison ten times longer than I imagined, how much time had actually passed. If I had, I might well have gone mad. So I never noticed, even though others all around us were aging and dying, that the Warden himself never aged a day more than I did in all of those 45 years that I was there."

I nodded. "Another vampire, then."

"Another vampire, perhaps, watching me, observing everything I did and didn't do for nearly half a century. I have often heard stories of other immortals walking the Earth, who are not vampires. I have never encountered one such, myself. Nonetheless, I have no idea what the man expected of me, J, nor whether I fulfilled his expectations of me or not."

"How could you?" I shrugged.

"I also didn't know, at the time, that he had served as Warden of that tiny, isolated prison under the Nazis, as well as the Communists, possibly back to before the time of King Carol II. Search though I may, by whatever means, I can find no record of his ever *not* being there."

"I wonder how he swung that," I said quietly.

She smiled. "The same way you 'swing' not having a driver's license, I suppose. The same way we both fed at the library this morning."

"Damn." I shook my head. "I never thought of using it for job security. I could be the mayor of this town—the governor of this state."

"A mayor or a governor," she asked, putting in her earrings, "who can never come out on a bright, sunny day to cut a ribbon and make a speech?"

"I never thought of that, either. You have a point—in fact, you've got a couple of points, but we'll explore that later. If the guy took it on the lam during the revolution in 1989, then what's the problem?"

She mused. "'On the lam'—I never heard that one. No doubt from the Icelandic, *lemja*. 'Beating feet,' as the vernacular would have it."

I laughed, but looked it up later and she was right.

"The problem—my problem—is that he stayed behind, this Warden, to intercept me, although what he wants from me, I have never learned."

"Look at yourself," I told her. She was, without question, the most beautiful thing I had ever seen. "What would any man want from you? What do I want from you, just as soon as we can get rid of our guests?"

"Our guests." She grinned, but waved away what I'd just said with a very eastern European gesture. "He is apparently not just any man, this Warden, but something different. We have met, on occasion we have even conversed. Never did I see in his eyes, my love, what I see in yours."

"Geez—a eunuch vampire. Dickless for all eternity. What a cruel fate!"

She laughed out loud that time. It was one of the nicest sounds I'd ever heard in my life. "But there can be no eunuch vampires. We heal."

"Indeed, we do." And I had a second appendix to prove it. "What do you think he wants?" It was by far the longest stalking case I'd heard of.

"I don't know, my love, and that's what frightens me. He has followed me everywhere—what do you say, 'dogging my steps'—for decades. Now I learn that he's followed me to North America, and I am afraid."

I'd taken care of more than one stalker during my career as an unlicensed private investigator and equalizer. Just how different could this be? I asked her, "So what's this guy's name when he's at home?"

"What an odd turn of phrase. I do not know what name he goes by, but I have heard, from scholars of the occult, that, in the Ancient Language, the Oldest Language, he is called 'Deabru,' which means 'Nightmare.'"

16: COUNCIL OF WAR

"Hypocrisy, the lie, is the true sister of evil, intolerance, and cruelty."—Raisa Gorbachev

New Prospect, it says here in this Japanese tourist brochure, has more restaurants, per capita, than any other city in the world. Why this should be so (I've never figured it out, myself), the brochure declines to vouchsafe. It's not why I moved here, but it's a reason I stay.

Among those restaurants, we're fortunate to have several good barbecue places and a couple of great ones. The oldest of these is Brother Lem's. Brother Lem is an oldtime Baptist preacher, and if he's as good at that as he is at barbecue, this whole damn town is going to heaven.

Surica and I were sitting in the kitchen again, freshly showered and in my case shaved, brewing up iced tea and making sure there was plenty of beer in the refrigerator. Fiddlestring's ears perked up when noise at the back door told us both that we had guests. Since it was still rainy and dark, I didn't have to duck and flinch as I let them in.

Before he was quite in the door, Quinn said, "I think we got the right thing, here, for the kind of day it is." He was carrying a big box of foil-covered containers, with styrofoam corners poking up here and there. I could have told from across the yard where it had come from.

Quyen followed him with a big old-fashioned leather briefcase. They took their jackets off and hung them up on pegs by the door to dry. She reached down and scratched the cat between the ears as he purred.

As we entered the kitchen, I could see that Surica had caught the wonderful scent and that she liked it. I hadn't asked her how long she'd been in the States, or whether she'd ever had barbecue before. Somehow it hadn't come up. I have a theory that vampires might be especially fond of the stuff (basing my conclusions on a field of one) because it reminds them of...well, of something else deep red and sweet.

"Surica Fieraru," I stood beside her. She was wearing jeans and a sweater, had her hair pulled back into a ponytail, and looked just swell. "These are my friends Tran Thi Thu-Quyen (we call her 'Quyen') and Quinlan Kowalski (we call him 'Quinn,' too). I know that sounds confusing, but don't worry, it'll only get more confusing as you go along."

Everybody chuckled politely. The cat turned and left the room.

"They know what I am," I added. "They figured it out all by themselves."

Handshakes were offered and accepted. "Quinn and Quyen are freelance scientific consultants. Usually I'm the one who asks them questions. I gather from Quinn that that's going to be different today."

"Lunch before questions," Quinn insisted, pouring himself a glass of tea from a carafe on the counter. He took containers from the box and set them out. "Pulled pork, ribs, chicken, brisket, sausage," he said as he did so, adding, "Hushpuppies, beans, cole slaw, and dill pickles."

I grinned. "All the basic food groups."

"Most of the time, he's a devout atheist," Quyen explained. "But he's very religious about food, especially when it comes from Brother Lem's."

"Hallelujah!" Quinn exclaimed.

I turned to get plates and silverware, but Surica had beaten me to it.

○

"So there's you," Quinn pointed a dill spear at me, "and your delightful new friend, here." He indicated Surica, who was just finishing off the last of the hushpuppies and pulled pork, and was licking barbecue sauce from her fingers like a veteran. "And suddenly the vampire population seems to have tripled." They hadn't had to guess this time; Surica had told them. "What's next, a pack of werewolves?"

I said, "There's no such thing as a werewolf, Quinn. There never was."

Surica nodded. "He's right." The two of us had agreed we wouldn't talk about Surica's life in the eighteenth and nineteenth centuries. To my two friends, for now, she was the girl I'd met in France, in 1944.

"How's that?" Quinn and Quyen said it at the same time.

I explained. "In some cultures, people who contracted the virus were thought to be like bats for some reason. I don't see it, myself. In others, they seemed to have the attributes of wolves. Rabid wolves, at that. In reality, there's only one virus and only one set of symptoms."

"How do you know all this stuff," Quyen looked skeptical, "if you've never met another vampire...well, that is, excepting Surica, here?"

"Because I've spent most of the last 65 years researching it."

Quinn: "Okay, so what you're saying is, you're a werewolf."

In a way, he was right. "What I'm saying is that I'm no more like a bat than I am like a wolf. Take a look at the constellations at night."

Quinn pretended to reel. "Whoa! Sudden change of subject!" He looked around at the others. "Damn good thing I had my seatbelt fastened!"

"Not a change of subject. Just consider: how much do any of the classic constellations really look like the things they're supposed to be: a club-wielding super hero, a pair of twins, a lady sitting in a chair..."

"There's the Big Dipper..." Quinn offered.

I nodded. "Some observers see it as a wagon or a bear. What I'm saying is that to some, people like me seem like bats—I don't know why—and to others, they seem more like wolves, although neither is true."

Quyen lit up. "I get it—just look at all the things different cultures think a rooster is hollering in the morning. Americans say 'cock-a-doo-dle-doo!' while the French would say, 'keekeerikee!' or something."

I grinned at Surica. "By george, I think they've got it."

Quyen said, "So you could be a *chupacabra*."

"Or a Sasquatch," Quinn answered.

Quyen looked doubtful. "He's a little small for a Sasquatch."

"Not where it counts, dear," said Surica.

○

"If nobody objects, I'm going to hypothesize that the guy asking people questions about J might be this 'Deabru' we've been talking about," Quinn told Surica. "Sure you don't know the guy by any other name?"

"I have tried to remember." She shook her head. "I know he must have had one, if only to be issued salary checks as Warden of that prison."

"Possibly going back as far as the 1890s," I said. "I'll bet those records have all been destroyed, along with all the Nazi and Communist records."

Surica seemed to stare into space. "There is a great deal that those who have ruled my country, usually against the will of the people, have to be ashamed of—and to greatly fear being punished for."

"Let's see." Quinn stood his old-fashioned briefcase upright on the counter, popped the brass fastener, and lifted the strap passing under the double handle. Reaching in, he pulled out what I recognized as a fairly large zippered pistol rug, and a square ballistic nylon envelope. He opened the latter and pulled out a small Toshiba laptop computer.

As we waited for it to boot, I asked, "What's in the pistol rug?" I'm not really much of a gun guy, but I've never failed to find them interesting.

Quinn unzipped the container and pulled out something that looked like it had come straight out of a western movie, all blued steel (although I learned later that the grip frame is made of aluminum) and dark, figured walnut grips. Not putting a finger on the trigger, he thumbed the hammer back until it clicked twice, then opened a little curved door on the right side of the frame, and rolled the cylinder until, click by click, five big cartridges, twice the length of one of my .45 ACPs and very nearly as big around, fell out into his waiting palm.

I'd probably seen the same thing done in a dozen horse operas.

"I know it's not the likeliest combat piece," he explained. "Slow to load and unload, slow to fire. But it'll stop a car, and it's what I've got, a Ruger Blackhawk .44 Magnum. You might say it's a first edition, the model known as the 'Flattop.'" It looked tiny in his big hand, like a kid's toy six-shooter. "With a six and a half inch barrel."

Surica asked, "Is it old?" It certainly didn't look particularly new. Both the muzzle and the cylinder seemed to have a lot of holster wear.

Quinn shook his head. "Not by the standards you're used to—as a European, I mean, not a vampire. The story is that, hounded by gun magazine writers and reloading experimenters, Smith & Wesson, a famous maker of double-action police revolvers, along with the ammunition side of Remington (who also made rifles and shotguns) were working on a powerful new pistol cartridge in 1956, based on an older, weaker .44 Special."

"1956," she mused. She'd been a prisoner then, for more than twelve years, and would be for another thirty-three. I still have no idea how she survived it. It was hard to fathom, even for another vampire.

"The new offering," Quinn continued, "to be called '.44 Magnum,' would be longer than the parent case, and run at higher pressures, even outperforming quite a number of rifle cartridges. The funny thing is that neither of the cartridges is actually a .44, but has an actual diameter of 0.429"—a true .43. Somehow hearing Dirty Harry whisper, 'But seein' as this here is a .43 Magnum, the world's most powerful handgun, and could blow your head clean off' wouldn't have been the same."

"Dirty Harry?" Surica's brow wrinkled.

"I'll explain later," I told her.

"Clint Eastwood," Quyen added, as if it explained everything.

"Ah!" responded Surica. Perhaps it did.

"The legend holds that an employee of Sturm-Ruger, who made a very different kind of revolver, single-action cowboy guns, is said to have found some fired cartridges in Remington's trash—although what he was doing in their trash is beyond me—and took them back to his company."

I said, "There are many reasons why this story could be complete bullshit."

"You could be right," Quinn agreed cheerfully. "Now where was I? Oh, yeah—his company, who built a single-action sixgun around the empties and beat Smith & Wesson to the market by several months in 1957.

"This gun was made in that year."

17: FACE RECOGNITION

"A good End cannot sanctify evil Means; nor must we ever do Evil, that Good may come of it."—William Penn

"Yes," my dentist said. "I'm ashamed to admit it, but I do have a couple of surveillance cameras at my office. Insurance company made me put them in—liability. Outside, too, where people park. Why do you ask?"

Holding the phone to my ear, I nodded at the others in the kitchen, indicating that there might be pictures of this Deabru character, when he'd shown up out of nowhere to interrogate my dentist.

"Because," I told T.W., "we're trying to find out more about this clown who's been asking questions about me. I have someone else here who's seen him—two someone elses, in fact, and another one who may have known him a long time ago. If you have photos, it might help a lot."

T.W. said, "Well, I have the disks, right here. Standard stuff. You can read them in any decent computer system. Would you care to come over and get them, or should I bring them to you, after office hours?"

It was fairly obvious which way he'd prefer. I gave it about five seconds' thought. "It'd probably be less crowded if you brought them over. I think there may even be some barbecue left. It's from Brother Lem's. There's nobody here but us chickens, T.W.—and a lovely young lady I'd sure like to introduce you to." Well, she looked like a young lady to me. She felt like one, too, for that matter. Was it Groucho Marx or George Burns who said, "You're only as old as the person you feel"?

He said, "And everybody there knows that you're...knows your secret."

"It's Quinn and Quyen," I told him, "the Kowalskis, who've played poker with you the first Thursday of every month for the past three years. They've known about me longer than you have." Anton played poker with us, too, but he didn't know, although I was beginning to wonder why. "As for the young lady, she has the same...secret that I do."

"The hell you say! Who does her teeth?"

O

"Okay, here's the part where I come into the waiting room after Dolly's decided that she's afraid of this guy and can't really deal with him." T.W. took another bite of the rib sandwich he'd composed and, totally fearless when it came to getting barbecue sauce in somebody else's keyboard, leaned closer to the monitor. "We could see his face a lot better if they hadn't mounted the damned cameras up so high."

"You're supposed to take your hat off when you come inside," I objected. I know, small farm town boy. If I looked my age, I'd be dead.

Quinn snorted. "Who knows from hat etiquette any more?"

"I doubt they ever did, in New Jersey," said Quyen.

"There is not one serious bone in any of your bodies." Surica complained. She'd been listening to us bantering back and forth for hours and apparently gotten tired of it. "You people are all so...American."

"Not all of us," said Quyen.

"Yeah, the sticker on her ass says 'Made in Ho Chi Minh City.'" Quinn.

I said, "It's how we've learned to solve problems, Surica. And it's what keeps us from screaming and throwing things. Forget that, or suppress it, you've got people on the rooftop with rifles, shooting at random pedestrians. Actually, we've got those, too—America, land of opportunity and diversity. You're sure this is the guy you knew as the Warden?"

She took a while to reply. "I am sorry, my love. I promise that I'll try to learn. This jocular method of yours seems to work, or we wouldn't be looking at these pictures now. And yes, that is the Warden—Deabru himself. Seeing him like this is probably why I became cross with you. It brings back certain memories I was much happier doing without."

"I hear that." Forty-five years, afraid, isolated, virtually buried, cold and starving every minute, surrounded everywhere by death. And this guy held the keys. It would have made me a bit testy, myself.

Or turned me into a standup comedian.

○

The next morning, the rain was back, so I didn't need my duster and Stetson. Thumb drive in hand, I went directly to see Anton at his office.

"So I wondered," I finished up my spiel, "if you could somehow get these photos into the Homeland Security face-recognition database." I don't like the fact that they have it—the whole thing makes me wonder why we bothered to fight the Nazis in Europe and Communists in Asia—but since they do, why not use it for good, instead of evil? Of course that's exactly the "reasoning" that perpetuates these things.

"He's been stalking a friend of mine. We know what he is, what he does, but not his real name. If it helps, he's probably an illegal immigrant."

So was Surica, for that matter.

Anton looked me in the eye. "You watch too much TV, Giff. In the first place, this generation of feds sees local law enforcement as the enemy, same as they view the people in general, only more so. As a consequence—and in the second place—the use of databases like that is highly restricted and closely monitored. This state may be about to lose its governor over an alleged misuse of the NCIC database."

I'd heard about that. Good riddance.

"It's true, the illegal immigrant angle might grease the skids a little, but I'll need more information, a lot more, before I can do anything."

I nodded. "Then I'll be your huckleberry."

"Huckleberry Hound?" he asked, confused.

"No. Val Kilmer. Doc Holliday. *Tombstone*."

"Oh, yeah. The little silver cup." He pushed himself away from the old oak table that served him as a desk, pulled his Glock .40 out of a drawer, and grabbed his jacket from a matching stand. "Let's take a walk."

I shrugged. "Okay."

I was surprised that our walk took us, not further into the town, as such excursions usually did, often over to Starbucks or someplace similar, but away from it, down to the river that runs alongside the city, where they've built a scenic concrete walk. People come here to pick wild asparagus when it's in season, and the kids like to catch crawdads at the edges of the stream. Presently, however, we had it to ourselves.

Anton said, "I just wanted the privacy to thank you properly, Giff."

He'd surprised me again. "Thank me?" I responded lamely.

He stopped and turned to face me. "For what you did for Priscilla. Our deal, though she denies it, is that I'm supposed to die in *her* arms. Thanks to you, buddy, life will go on being worth living. Don't deny it. I know exactly what you did, Giff, how you did it, and why it worked."

"But how—" I was honestly dumbfounded.

"Guy works nights, doesn't need much sleep, can't bear the light of day, wears sunblock, a long coat, and a big floppy hat, seems most active on heavily overcast days like this, and is sickened by the smell of garlic—Pris caught that one a long time ago—and heals terminal cancer in ten minutes. Gimme a break. I am a detective, after all."

"Sure, Anton. You're the Chief of Detectives."

"I'm chief of *three* detectives, including myself. And you're a vampire."

I sighed. "How long have you known?"

"Ten years, maybe more. Once I figured it out, I kept an eye on you, but you didn't appear to be hurting anybody. You came to me more frequently with information than for favors—in fact, this may be the first time you've asked me for anything. Bodies weren't showing up in the river with dual punctures in their necks. In fact, N.P. has a lower crime rate than it has any right to, statistically, a minutely higher life expectancy, and noticeably fewer nasty diseases. Maybe it isn't all of it your doing, pilgrim, but you're sure as hell doing something."

We walked on in silence for a while. Then: "Not the first time I've asked for a favor, Anton. There was the business with the library books."

He laughed. Ten or twelve years ago, a new Chief of Police had decided to help the city library by getting warrants to search the homes of the desperate criminals whose library books were overdue. I had two, but I figured I couldn't afford to have a bunch of cops and librarians rummaging through my closets and turning my drawers upside down. Anton and some of his brother officers had convinced the idiot they had better things to do. He'd backed off grudgingly, and at the request of somebody he would never remember, resigned shortly afterward.

And so did the head librarian.

"You knew about me—your wife knew—and yet you didn't arrest me."

"Well, at first I thought you were like those poseurs in Denver, playing weekend sucky-neck to compensate for their cubicle farm jobs. But the deeper I looked, the more I became certain that you were—that you are—the real thing. And it isn't against the law to be a vampire."

"I guess that makes us even in a way. You kept my secret, and I was able to help your Priscilla. Of course it's not like I had any choice."

"About being a vampire? I understand that."

"No, I mean Priscilla. I know she means everything to you. She ought to. She deserves to. She's everything a wife and mother—a woman in general—ought to be. The fact is, I was always a little envious—"

"Was," Anton seized upon the word. "And now? This new girlfriend of yours—the one my wife is dying to meet—she's one, too, isn't she?"

I didn't bother asking how he knew I had a new girlfriend. He'd just give me a smug expression and tell me he was a detective again. "A wife and mother? Not yet, but I have hopes. A woman in general? I'll say she is! But no details, please. I'm not the kind to kiss and tell."

"But you are the kind who will make jokes on his deathbed—provided that he ever dies, that is. You know exactly what I'm asking, Giff."

"Is Surica (that's her name, by the way) a vampire? Yes she is, Anton."

"What I wanted to know, is she The Woman? By which I mean the one who—"

"Brought me over. Elementary, my dear Varick, that she is. As silly as it sounds, she's my sire. I promise I'll tell you and the mem'sahib all about it sometime, since you seem to know everything else."

He said, "So how old are you, Giff—just curious, don't mean to pry."

"You're a detective, Anton, you were born to pry. I will be 90 years old this December 15, born in 1920, brought over in 1944. My girlfriend, she's just a little bit older, born on the Romanian-Serbian border in 1711, brought over in 1728. But the character we're looking for, the guy who's looking for us, is the genuine longevity champ."

"Oh, yeah? How old is he?"

"We don't know. In some ways, we're both a little afraid to find out. The oldest name he's known by is from the oldest language in Europe, maybe even from a time when it was the *only* language in Europe."

"Basque."

"Say, Anton, you really *are* a detective!"

18: LIFE GOES ON

"The face of evil is always the face of
total need." —William S. Burroughs

"*B*ut now he's disappeared," she wailed, "and I want my money!"
The trouble with having a job is that it continues to need
doing—or insist on being done—even when you'd rather be
doing other things.

"Please try to remain calm, Mrs. Gumbeiner," I said, riffling through
the thick manila folder she had handed me. "You just tell me the facts. I'll
make some notes and give you an idea of what I can do."

After sailing along more or less calmly for quite a number of years, my
personal boat had been rocked recently by a number of events and revela-
tions I didn't really have a handle on yet. My "family"—by which I mean
the circle of individuals who know and understand my "condition" had
suddenly more than doubled, with the addition of four Varicks, Anton,
Priscilla, Patrick, and Amber (all of whom, it turned out, had known
about me all along) and, above all, lovely, lithe Surica.

In many ways, this was a good thing. Quinn and Quyen Kowalski and
my dentist T.W. Beemort are fine folks, good company, and T.W. has a
charming inclination to try and fill an inside straight. But if you grew up
in the very model of a small American town, like I did, and the life you've
lived for the past 65 years has been as solitary as mine, the more people
sitting around the Thanksgiving table the better.

"I've got myself the very best attorney in Denver," my would-be client informed me. "He won me sole custody of my son Augustus and an
extremely reasonable settlement, considering. After all, I'd abandoned a
promising career to marry Morton and carry and raise the child the man
thoughtlessly fathered on me. And then, when Morton disappeared, utterly without a trace, he sent me straight to you. The attorney, I mean."

"And you'd like me to find him." I could do that if I had to.

"No, I want you to hunt him down like the animal he is, and—"

"Kill him?" Yes, sometimes a sense of humor is your only life preserver.

She blinked. "Don't be ridiculous!" Maybe I'd been wrong about her and
was about to face moral condemnation. "How can he pay me if he's dead?"

Hell hath no fury like a woman spermed.

There was a downside to my broadened social life to be considered, however. No matter how good or kindly or well-meaning my friends and family might try to be, wasn't it Mark Twain who observed that two people can keep a secret if one of them is dead? Or perhaps it was Benjamin Franklin. Or Catherine and Allison Pierce. Loose lips sink ships—and, historically, they've also gotten vampires burned at the stake.

I said, "I know that it isn't any of my business, but if you could answer a couple of questions, it might make it easier for me to do my job."

"Well..." she answered.

I put my hands on the desk and leaned forward. "In what way is it good for your young son to grow up knowing that his father had to be physically *forced* to support him? If I'd been a kid, knowing that, it would have ruined my whole life. Mightn't it be better just to let go and start over on your own? After all, there is that career you had, right?"

A high school teacher I had once said that the hardest lesson to learn in life, growing up, is that other people are real. As real as you are. Some individuals never do manage to learn it. The second hardest thing, he said, is letting them go. Most people never learn that.

"Are you kidding me? I was a telephone receptionist at a tire factory that got shut down! Anyway, just what right do you have to ask me—"

"None whatever, Mrs. Gumbeiner, none whatever. I thought that I had explained that. I'm just trying to understand." She was getting angry. I could hear her heart pound, see the pulses at her throat and temple, smell the alarm pheromones she was perspiring into my office. "Okay, you say that you were granted sole custody of your son Augustus. And I see that you have a restraining order against your ex-husband."

"Yes," she said. "So?"

I couldn't lean forward further. "So why should he pay a hundred percent of the kid's support if he shares zero percent of the kid's life?"

"But, but, but—" Outrage. I'd have to air the office out later.

I pressed on. "If you have a hundred percent of the kid, then why shouldn't you pay for a hundred percent of his upbringing? Of course I guess you'd have to get a job, and that might affect your alimony payments. Wouldn't it make more sense to share the kid and his support fifty-fifty?"

As a vampire, I try to maintain as low a profile as I can, without living in a cave somewhere and eating worms and bark. You might say that I am *on* the grid, but not *of* it. Naturally, I avoid politics like the plague, but that certainly doesn't mean I don't have my own opinions.

The trouble here, of course, was judges, full of law school drivel in no way connected with real life, and two centuries of the insanity of justification by precedent, giving away other people's money, and destroying their lives, a process bound to continue until the American people rediscover the fact that a lamppost can serve more than one purpose.

A wise man once asked, "What shall we have accomplished when we have made a law?" Or words to that effect. He goes on to point out that those who agree with the new law are most likely "obeying" it already, before it's ever passed. Meanwhile, those who don't agree with it will either obey it grudgingly, which is very dangerous in the long run, especially in a democracy, where nothing is ever really settled, or they will break it surreptitiously, a particular specialty of yours truly.

What we will really have accomplished, says the wise man, is to have given more jobs to cops, and bought more guns and clubs—and these days, TV cameras. If law really worked, there'd be no need for it.

But above and beyond everything were questions swirling through my mind about Surica, and what things would be like, now that we were back in each other's lives. Having her around felt absolutely magical, and all I could hope was that it wasn't too intolerable for her, either. Potentially, we had more future together than any ten average couples—we already had a record-breaking past—and I hoped, more than anything, that what seemed to me like a fragile miracle could last.

I would do anything in my power to make it happen.

But before I could get to cogitating any of that, there was this pesky necessity to eat, wear something besides road-killed squirrel skins, have a roof over my head, wheels under my feet, and various other means of shielding myself from outrageous fortune's slings and arrows.

Not that I was on my way to the poor house, exactly. Having seen Europe at the end of the war—World War II, I mean, not all those other wars that the highly civilized Europeans seem to have so many of—I started buying gold and silver whenever I could, and investing in the sort of slow, steady growth that only an immortal might benefit from.

I suppose it's fair to say that if I were to stop working for a living, I wouldn't exactly go hungry. When you get over that first thrill of discovering that you're going to live more or less forever, you begin to realize—or at least I did—that time really is money.

I had some early help in this. The elementary school I attended in my home town participated in the "Bank Day System," invented, odd as it may seem, by the murder mystery writer Rex Stout. Every Thursday (in my school, anyway) the kids would all hand over whatever pennies they had to their teacher, who made entries in a book for them and let the resulting envelope full of coins be taken to the bank to draw interest.

I reckon that if I still had that account, it would be worth about half a billion dollars, but it would be hard to get at, with my being missing in action and presumed dead. Happily, I cleared the account out the day I graduated from high school, and when I got to England, preparatory to D-Day, bought a little bar of gold—illegal in the good old U.S. of A.—I carried with me through was left of the war.

As soon after the war as I could manage, and before I worked my way back to the States, I left that gold bar in an interest-bearing account in Switzerland. Later on, I split the account, then split it again, and now have fifty or sixty accounts spread all over the planet.

All it takes is time.

I have some other investments, too—I put every dime I can into whatever company is leading the pack in battery design and I was lucky to see transistors for what they would eventually become—but most of my money comes from slow and steady sources. The same thing would work for shorter-lived people, too, if their governments didn't get so greedy.

Surica provided for herself in pretty much the same way, except that she didn't have much time immediately following the war. Instead, she started investing in the 18th century and truly is a billionaire now.

A really quiet billionaire.

By now, I had a lot of money of various kinds stashed, hidden, or right out in plain sight in a lot of different places, but you have to keep the momentum going, and if you don't work in some way—or maybe this is the small town boy thinking—then in some way you start to die.

So I answer the telephone, I read my e-mail, and I examine what the U.S. Snail brings to me every day, exactly as if I were only a paycheck and a half away from bankruptcy, just like everybody else in America.

And that's how I happened to be sitting at my desk now, listening to this woman on the other side of it complaining that she had been guaranteed freedom from having to earn a living, just like everybody else, by a magistrate who had generously bestowed upon her about a hundred and twenty percent of her soon-to-be ex-husband's future income. Some of it was alimony. A whole lot more of it was child support.

"Look, Mr...." She consulted an envelope she had written on.

"Gifford," I said. "J Gifford."

"Mr. Gifford, do you want this job or not?"

I leaned back in my chair. "No, Mrs. Gumbeiner, I do not want this job. And if you have any sense at all, neither do you. Your ex-husband has just lost everything that means anything to a man, his home, his family, and his job, I presume. The guy's become a fugitive, living in hiding, sort of a one-man Witness Protection Program. You divorced him, that's what it says here in these papers, anyway. It was pretty clearly your choice. Whatever it was he did or failed to do, he's being punished. Why attempt to continue a relationship that you've rejected?"

"Well, I never!" She was wrong about that. She had at least once. Now she got up, stiff all over with anger, slung her big purse over her shoulder like an M1 Garand, and headed for the front door. "This isn't over, not by a long shot. I'm going to talk to my attorney about you!"

I had arisen, too. Chivalrous reflex established in childhood. "Good idea. I'm planning to talk to him myself, in just a minute or two."

There are worse bloodsuckers in the world than vampires.

19: A LITTLE KNIFE MUSIC

"Right, temporarily defeated, is stronger than
evil triumphant."—Martin Luther King, Jr.

"So this is what you do for a living," Surica said. She meant the would-be client earlier that afternoon. She'd been listening from my study.

I said, "I've dealt with worse. If I waited until Mary Poppins showed up to hire me, or Mother Teresa, I'd be living in a cardboard box."

"This is definitely not a cardboard box," she observed. The bedroom was large, well-lit in the daytime—more special glass—but very private at the same time, thanks to good architecture. Ordinarily I didn't spend much time here, but I enjoyed having it nonetheless.

"Arts and Crafts, from the 1920s," I told her. "I like it, too." It was the main reason I'd chosen to stop wandering and put down roots in New Prospect. That and the fact that it was near Denver, but not in Denver.

"You never told me about Sava Savanovic," I observed. We had just made love for the third time in an hour. It may be good to be the king, as Mel Brooks tells us, but it's a hell of a lot better to be a vampire.

Surica said, "Who?" We were smoking cigarettes that she'd brought with her. I'd never tried it before, although most guys back in the 40s did, but I was giving it a try now. What was it going to do, kill me?

"Or maybe what," I said. "Or where. I won't actually know until you tell me. It's the name you made our reservation for at Boiling Oil."

The good thing about being a smoking vampire is that the virus protects you from needing to cough or feeling sick the way you're supposed to the first time you smoke. The bad thing is that it wasn't doing anything for me, either, any more than cannabis or opiates do. I wondered why Surica stuck with such a dirty habit, but I didn't ask her.

Not then, anyway.

"Oh, that! It is a joke, darling, a vampire joke, like 'Joe sent me' or 'Kilroy was here'—as if you made a reservation for Sam Marlowe."

"Who?" I knew what she meant but I wanted to hear her explain it. I loved to listen to her talk, like Boris's Natasha, but a prettier voice.

She frowned. "Philip Spade, then. This is right?"

"About as close as Nero Goodwin or Archie Wolfe." Momentarily I wondered if there had ever been vampires in Montenegro. "But you were saying..."

"Sava Savanovic is most famous vampire in Serbian folklore. More in his own time than Romania's Vlad Tepes." Whenever she talked about the old country, her accent became noticeably thicker. "He is said to have dwelt in old mill on river Rogacica in village of Zarozje, municipality of Bajina Basta. Is said he used to kill millers coming to mill their grain so as to drink their blood. Look it up. Is on Wikipedia."

I folded my arms across my chest. "So is the Loch Ness Monster."

She ignored me. "Although Savanovic is usually said to have been first Serbian vampire, there are claims of earlier vampire in Serbian folklore, a man, Petar Blagojevic from Veliko Gradiste, who died in 1724."

"Only four years before you were turned. How truly strange. Or maybe he faked his death and lived to become the fortieth governor of Illinois."

She ignored me. "Thirteen years after I was born—is sounding more sinister that way. Petar Blagojevic and everything about him came to popular European attention at that time, only under name Peter Plogojowitz, for some reason. Is earliest example of vampire hysteria. I believe it was his...call them successors who sired me, or perhaps some collateral 'relation' of Sava Savanovic. I myself have been to that watermill upon two occasions, once before war with Hitler and once again just before I was captured and imprisoned by Communists. Is property of Jagodic family these days and is usually called *Jagodica vodenica*."

"Let me guess: Jagodic's watermill. I go to see the meteor crater at Winslow, Arizona every year, myself. It takes a hell of a lot of sunblock."

"Very good, lovely man. I shall put gold star on your foreskin."

I barely stifled a laugh. "Unh...I believe you mean forehead, Surica."

"I shall reward whatever parts of you I feel may merit it, my love. Where was I? Oh, yes: famous watermill was functional until late 1950s, when it was closed by government. Tourists come, sometimes, to see authentic 'vampire mill.' Their numbers slowly dwindle every year."

○

I am perfectly willing to work during the daytime, given certain precautions, but nobody seems to want me to. People do what they're ashamed to have other people seeing them do in the night, and people who need to defend themselves from the first kind of people need people like me, night people, to defend them. It isn't so much that the night belongs to a private eye, as a private eye belongs to the night.

Which is why I was lying on the roof of a client's garage, just below the peak, keeping both of my private eyes on the back of a house very nearly as nice as my own. I did envy them their location just a little, a classy, inconspicuous neighborhood on Tanfoglio Lane, just off Bicentennial, on the placid shore of the thoroughly artificial Lake Nottingham. The father of the family who lived there was an extremely well-paid "executive engineer" (that's what it said on his card, anyway) for an international electronic outfit whose name you'd recognize.

The trouble was with his daughter, sixteen, physically precocious, sweet-smelling, with pale blond hair, eyes the color of well-washed denim, and the peaches and cream face of an angel. She was actually a pretty nice kid, despite being aware that she was beautiful. I was tempted to bite her myself; I understood the guy they were all upset about.

To a degree, anyway.

Precious daughter, it developed, had gone to an innocuous-sounding teenage party at a school friend's house a week ago, a party that she probably shouldn't have gone to. Wearing a dress that she probably shouldn't have worn, she had had a couple of drinks that she probably shouldn't have had. But the "probably shouldn't haves" didn't end there.

In her state of alcohol-induced amiability, she'd ended up on a broken-down couch in the middle of the party for a couple of hours, playing what we used to call "tonsil hockey" and assorted similar games with a dropout from Von Mises U. seven years older than she was. It turned out that his name was Wayne, he was well known to the local police—mostly as the son of a city councilman who owned a business that employed several hundred New Prospectians and fed their families—and he made a bad habit of cruising high school parties like this one.

Wayne's next move would have been to drag her off to a bedroom or, better yet, to his car, and give her something other than his tongue to suck on. We found out later that he'd done exactly that with many another high school girl. But, accidentally in the nick of time, a couple of the daughter's best friends forever had done the dragging, driving her home with certain tips on how to fool your folks about what you drank, as well as a number of classical high school hangover remedies.

I'm certainly no wimp, but I will never be able to look at a bottle of butterscotch ice cream topping in quite the same way, ever again.

Or leeks.

Later that night, the guy had shown up on the second-story balcony of the house, through a tragic miscalculation on his part, at her folks' enormous bedroom picture window that ordinarily looked out at the mountains. What Romeo had seen, instead of the teenager of his dreams in her babydoll negligee, was the double muzzle of her father's custom Browning Superposed 12 gauge trap and skeet gun—purely for sporting purposes, don't you know old chap, pip pip—just as it went off.

The police, who could find no trace of the guy—principally because they hadn't looked—had decided to end this threat to peace and civil order by confiscating the father's shotgun. Twenty-four hours later, after a second midnight visitation, warded off with a putter this time, dear old Dad had gone straight to his golfing buddy Anton Varick. Anton had sent him to me. I persuaded the properties and evidence guy to give me the shotgun, leaving him with the distinct impression that the confiscating cops had come to claim it for their very own. With any luck they'd spend the rest of their lives guarding empty parking lots in Moose Jaw, Saskatchewan—or working for the F.B.I.

My real job was to catch the mad midnight masher in the act and encourage him to modify his undesirable behavior—with prejudice. I could do that, with bells on. But the first thing I was sure to do was to inconspicuously sniff around the balcony and the place on the patio below where the guy had fallen. (How the client had missed him at that range with a shotgun, I had no idea.) I not only have a better sense of smell than many a dog—not necessarily a good thing; the vast majority of odors in the world are bad—I have an olfactory memory so acute that, if I ran into this guy fifty years from now in a shopping mall in DeFuniak Springs, Florida, I'd know who it was I was smelling.

Now, here I lay on the garage roof, just below the ridge line, waiting. There were raccoons in this neighborhood, and a female fox with her young. At some distance I could smell mule deer and a big old owl.

In due course, I heard him in the alley behind the house, making noises like a steam locomotive with gravel in its hubcaps. He'd been hurt pretty bad in the fall, and hadn't been in great shape to begin with. He probably thought he was running on silent. Taking a peek—it was a moonless night, but like broad daylight to me—over the crest of the garage roof, I could see that he was a little worse for wear. He had a broad bandage holding his nose on his face (or his eyes together) and a cast on his left arm, probably from the fall he'd taken.

I had smelled him before I'd seen or heard him.

He was the guy.

He was wearing jeans, an old gray sweatshirt, and a watchcap. He also had a fairly big knife hanging in a scabbard from his belt, a Buck "General," at one time, about the only large knife made in America. He got in through the back gate and stealthed his way up to the house. By now he knew where daughter's bedroom window was. What he didn't know is that she was sleeping snugly in her Disney's Pocahontas sleeping bag in her mother's sewing room at the front of the big house.

"Thinking of committing a felony?" I asked conversationally as I alighted silently on the balcony beside him. It had been a sixty foot jump. And no, it isn't flying. He let out a little "yip!" and tried to turn and draw his knife at the same time, a trick difficult enough with both arms working. I kept him turning past the point where he'd intended to stop, taking the Buck from his hand as that part of him went by. With my other hand, I grabbed him by the seat of his baggies, bunching them good and hard at the crotch so he wouldn't slip out of them.

I lifted him over the two-by-four rail like a crane and held him, head down, over the patio where he'd already broken his arm and nose. "Would you rather talk," I pretended to ask, "or should I let you go? It's only a dozen feet, but that concrete down there looks really hard."

"Talk! Talk!" he tried to yell and whisper at the same time.

"Good idea to be quiet. I gave her father back his shotgun." The words sounded almost as sweet to me as, "Oh good! My dog found the chainsaw!"

Swinging him back in, I set him on his feet and made him unfasten his belt. I could see and smell that he'd wet himself. What I wanted was the scabbard; I meant to keep the knife. I also took the belt so that he had to stand there, holding up his pants with his one good hand. The knife was okay. I sheathed it and stuck it in the back of my waistband.

"Now here's the way it is, Wayne. You appear to have a problem respecting the personal space—not to mention the virginity—of others. There are a lot of places I could send you for that. The state prison at Canyon City, for example, where you'll learn about personal space the hard way, and find out how you've been making the girls feel."

If his whimper had any semantic content, I couldn't tell.

I went on, "I could make you kill yourself—with this knife, say—but then it would be evidence, and I'm planning to add it to my collection."

"Oh, God! Please don't kill me!"

"I didn't say I would kill you. I said I might make you kill yourself."

"That's no improvement!"

"No, it isn't, is it? So here's what we'll do, instead..."

20: BLOWIN' IN THE WIND

*"The greatest minds are capable of the greatest vices as
well as of the greatest virtues."*—Rene Descartes

"*Y*ou let him go?" Both men said the same thing at once.

Before I could answer, the waitress brought our order. Gigantic cinnamon rolls swimming in buttery icing for them. Chicken fried steak and hashbrowns for me, four eggs over medium. Maybe a cinnamon roll after that. It had been a long night, and now it was another of the cold, blustery rainy days we'd been having. Strong, hot coffee all around.

Anton drinks his black like me. You can't drink station house coffee all night, the way you have to, sometimes, if you load it up with sugar and fat—which is exactly what the client happened to be doing now: two spoons of sugar and three little cups of "mouse milk"—what the Varick kids had called restaurant servings of half and half.

"No, I didn't exactly let him go," I told Anton and his golfing friend. It was the next morning. The three of us were having coffee and accessories at Uneeda Lunch Cafe, Est. 1912. The place was old, with hardwood floors and its original tin ceilings. "Believe it or not, there is this real, live, actual monastery up in Snowmass, near Aspen."

The client nodded. He cut himself a bit of cinnamon roll, mopping icing off the plate. "I think I've heard about that. Something on TV. Trappists?"

"No, that's in Colorado Springs," Anton told him. "I had to go down there once, years ago, to take custody of a perpetrator who erroneously believed that the law couldn't touch him in a place like that."

Outside, people wearing raincoats and carrying umbrellas hurried by on the sidewalk, occasionally illuminated by flashes of lightning. Some stopped when they saw the light and warmth inside the restaurant. Even for a vampire, it was a swell place to be on a rotten day like this.

I chuckled. "Sanctuary, is it?" And when Anton nodded, laughing behind the big napkin he was wiping his mouth with, I added, "I had a hunch."

Anton grimaced. The client was bewildered. Probably never heard of Quasimodo.

"I suggested to our party rapist that he go there for a while—a couple of years—to confess and contemplate his sins and make proper atonement. I'm pretty sure the monks down there can help him with that. They'll keep him busy, anyway. He was so grateful he left me this."

From my coat, I pulled the big Buck General #120 hunting and camp knife I'd brought to show them and laid it on the table. It had a fairly thick seven and a half inch Bowie-shaped blade with a "clipped point" (which is what made it a Bowie) and a fuller, or "blood-gutter" ground into each side along the back. The handle was black phenolic or something like it. The double guard with its red spacer and the pommel were a highly polished aluminum, and there was the heavy black leather sheath. For a long time, the 50s and the 60s, it had been the only truly big knife manufactured in America. Thousands of them had been sent by worried parents to sons in Vietnam. Nifty. I'd always wanted one.

The client looked down at the table, horror in his eyes. "You didn't—"

I could see Anton considering the same thing. The waitress came by and filled our coffee cups again before I could give them an answer and relieve their tension, which, to be honest, I'd sort of been enjoying.

"No, but I certainly thought hard about it. Where he's going, he won't need them. But rapists, deprived of their implements, often find other implements, and he won't be thinking much about women, in any case."

"He won't?" The client looked confused. Anton just looked curious.

"No, he won't. I persuaded the guy to give women up for a while." I tucked the knife back into my inside coat pocket. "And Anton, here, will tell you that I can be a fairly persuasive individual when I need to."

"You can?" the client asked.

"He can," said Anton.

"Yes," I said, "I can."

O

Patrick said, "The truth: you cured my mother's cancer, didn't you?"

To our right, the ever-peculiar Chickn Bitz emporium filled that end of the local mall with the overwhelming smell of boiling cooking oil. All you can eat for fifty bucks, or some similar kind of deal, exclusive to those who have taken Jesus as their personal savior. I have always thought it was an extremely bad idea to mix religion with business. I wondered what kind of deal they would have offered a vampire.

A chicken-fried stake?

On the other hand, the ambience here had to be better than at the other end, where perfume stores and bath shops collaborated with the odor of burned coffee from an enterprise calling itself "Leaves and Beans," to violate the Geneva Convention against the use of chemical weapons.

From the speakers, high overhead, we couldn't avoid listening to a bubbly, lighthearted, Muzak-style interpretation of "Blowin' in the Wind."

How many malls must a man walk down...

Just now, Patrick Varick walked beside me, along one of the longer axes of New Prospect's Rocky Mountain Mall, a sort of pitiful thing these days, with every other shopfront chained and shuttered, thanks to a national economy mortally wounded by both political parties. To Surica, of course, given a personal background of misery and privation exceeding even that of the rest of Soviet-era Romania, the place probably looked like Disneyland. She shopped ecstatically as I tagged along.

Patrick had called my cell and joined us.

I raised my eyebrows. The boy's father must not have told him about our recent talk. I stopped, not wanting to get too far ahead of Surica, who had gotten sucked over the event horizon of a women's shoe store.

"Here I thought you just wanted to come and ogle my new girlfriend before you head back to the Academy. You gotta admit, she's plenty ogleable."

Patrick was insistent. "Don't deny it, J. I know what you are. I know *exactly* what you are. It seems like I've always known. It was obvious. It was also excruciating. Here I was, a little kid whose father's best friend, my 'uncle,' was a real live vampire, but who couldn't brag to any of his friends—um, unless you object to being called—"

"An 'undead American'?" Political correctness had come to the United States Air Force Academy earlier than to most other places. "Or maybe you think I might prefer 'reflection deprived' or 'differently cuisined'?"

"'Hemoglobinically challenged.'" He laughed. "How about a vampire with—"

I shook my head. "With a heart of gold?"

"With a heart, anyway. Maybe a soul, too, like Angel on *Buffy the Vampire Slayer*. I don't know how to thank you, J. And I'm talking for Amber, as well. She knows about you, too, see? She'd tell you herself, but I just put her on a plane back to college. Our mother's going to live."

I sighed, partly wondering when lovely Surica was going to free herself from the spider web no woman can resist. It was way past lunchtime, and, not very far away, I could smell a tiny little hole in the wall shop that peddled the best damned miso soup in all of New Prospect.

Like I said, food: my favorite dish.

He said, "Your girlfriend—you're right, she's damned ogleable. Is that a Russian accent she has, or what? Maybe it's Transylvanian. She's a vampire like you, isn't she? I don't know how I know, but I know."

The kid knew too much, but had never had trouble keeping his mouth shut.

"Romanian," I said. "Surica's Romanian, originally. Look, Patrick, your dad and I have had this talk already. No expressions of gratitude of any kind are required. It's just this simple, really: I love your mother, too, in a nauseatingly wholesome, brotherly kind of way. And I owe her, a lot. You guys, the four of you Varicks, are the only family I have. You can thank me by not telling anybody else, if you can avoid it."

"You've got it, Unc." He winked. Just then, Surica emerged from the shoestore carrying a pair of big plastic bags full of cardboard boxes.

"Okay," she told us, looking extremely pleased with herself. "I'm finished for now. And I'm famished. What's for lunch? Is that miso I smell?"

The overhead had just broken out into a jaunty, upbeat version of "Eve of Destruction." I should probably have paid better attention to that.

○

Patrick exchanged a few polite words with Surica, then, possibly sensing that we wanted to be alone—or maybe it had more to do with getting back to the Air Academy—excused himself. We took Surica's treasure over to the food court, bought a couple of bowls of miso, some crispy noodles to have with it, and a family order of yakatori to share.

We talked. There was a shop near the entrance that didn't sell anything but chocolate in one form or another. Surica told me she was crazy about chocolate, one reason, she said, she'd chosen that fondue place for our first meeting in sixty-five years. Sometimes it feels as if my brain won't function without my Minimum Daily Requirement of chocolate. I wondered if all vampires are like that, or it was just us.

Surica: "You'll never believe what I found in that shoe store, my love!"

"Six-inch stilettos," I ventured, "with padlocked ankle straps."

"Silly," she replied. "How could a person walk in something like that?"

She knew perfectly well. She had slipped one shoe off and was toe-playing with my ankle under the table. Playing it straight, I said, "They're not meant for walking, sweetheart. Not very much, anyway."

"I see," she replied. "Perhaps I should reconsider, then."

I said, "Perhaps you should, my dear. But I seriously doubt that you'll find anything like that in New Prospect, especially at the mall."

"How very sad. A vanilla mall. Is that why they're going out of business?"

I laughed. They'd had a Frederick's of Hollywood here, but it hadn't lasted. And Victoria's Secret is that her stuff is pathetically ordinary.

We continued eating, me thinking thoughts that only began with six-inch stilettos with padlocked ankle straps, and, well, who knew what she was thinking. The way she looked around at the sparse crowd, it was more than possible that another trip to the library was in order.

Suddenly, she froze, transfixed at something she was seeing over my shoulder. "Don't turn," she whispered hoarsely. "It's him—the Warden!"

I did turn, but by that time, he was gone.

21: DANGER FOR LUNCH

"The sad truth is that most evil is done by people who never make up their minds to be good or evil."—Hannah Arendt

I couldn't see the man who'd frightened Surica.

But I could smell him.

Leaping out of my chair, I did something I had never done before. In full view of whatever people there were to see it—admittedly not very many on a weekday Depression afternoon—I ran, as fast as I could.

Following my nose, I crossed the food court at around forty miles and hour, ducking, dodging, even leaping over chairs and tables, and was out through one of the heavy doors in an instant—it took longer to get that damned door opened, adjusted as it had been to resist the Colorado prairie wind, as it had to run across the food court—and onto the opposite side of the mall from which we'd parked the PT Cruiser.

Hopping up into the heavy luggage carrier mounted on somebody's Land Rover, I steadied myself by clutching at a lamppost it had been parked too close to. It says here Colorado has twice the number of SUVs that are average in America. New Prospect has twice as many as that.

I looked around, still smelling the apparition that was haunting my lady-love, but unable to see him or very much of anything else in the horrible glare of sunlight that had crashed down on my head. I was dressed properly for daytime outdoors, but it was still a shock, like emerging from a movie theater in the middle of the afternoon. When I climbed back down, I noticed that I'd left finger dents in the metal pole.

I followed the scent—somehow it reminded me of boiled turnips—to the middle of the mostly empty parking lot and lost it. The guy had obviously gotten into a car and driven away somewhere. But why had he exposed himself like that in the first place? It had to mean something.

I had a sudden, scary thought, and reentered the mall at only a slightly more sedate pace. Sure enough, it had all been a well-planned and timed diversion. Surica was still sitting at the little table where I'd abandoned her so precipitously. But now, sitting on either side of her were, respectively, a uniformed mall-monkey and a city cop I knew.

I plunked myself into the fourth chair, opposite Surica, and said "Hello, boys," cheerfully. To Surica, I said, "What's going on here, sweetheart?"

People from eastern Europe tend to have the same attitude toward police officers that western Americans display toward diamondback rattlesnakes and black widow spiders. They have their reasons. At the moment, my girlfriend looked immensely relieved that I had come back to her.

"They claim that they are acting for your immigration authorities. They claim I am an illegal alien, but they are carrying no documents to justify it. They wanted me to come with them, but I know what that means. I managed to persuade them to sit here and be quiet, but I can't seem make them forget and go away. I've never had that trouble before."

I pushed the rent-a-cop a little. A young skinny guy sporting a flattop and bad skin, his mind was not as soft as he looked. Somehow, something had hardened him from the outside. He absolutely couldn't be persuaded about leaving Surica alone, so I had to come around the back way.

"You know," I began as pleasantly and conversationally as I could, "I've always wanted to ask one of you private mall security guys a question."

"Go ahead and ask." He looked at me exactly as if he were not under the influence of another mind, although the fact was undeniable. It was just as if a tower of Jell-O had steel scaffolding built around it.

"Okay," I replied, keeping my tone light. "Why would anybody ever choose to work for an employer that dressed them up like this, in a clown suit with a big shiny badge and an equipment belt, made them as conspicuous as all get-out, and then denied them the basic means of self-defense?"

"What?" Was it mind-control or just natural stupidity? And did it matter?

I tried to keep exasperation out of my voice. Surica was watching me intently. "Why wear a shoot-me-first suit, but no gun to go with it?"

"Oh, that." He sounded a little sad. "I guess because I need the job."

I nodded. "I hear that. You're making minimum wage, here, right? You'd like to make more money? Of course you would." I pulled out one of my business cards and took a ballpoint from his shirt pocket. "I want you to go to this address, and ask for Moe, the manager. Moe owes me a favor. If I ask him to, he'll give you a job for at least twice the rate you make now, probably with more hours. Buy yourself a nice car, get yourself a girl, have a better life than you were headed for."

I gave him back his pen, and the card.

The kid lit up. "Gee, thanks, mister. I'll go first thing end of shift."

I looked at his nametag. "Do it now, Kevin. Think about that car. Think about that girl. They're both out there somewhere waiting for you."

"I don't know..." he hesitated.

"Kevin, life is too short."

He got up. "You're right, mister! I'll do it!" And he was gone.

I turned to Surica. "My old friend Moe—he's from India and it's short for something long and unpronounceable—runs a chain of dirty book stores. I saved him from being kidnapped by his relatives and forcibly married. He actually sells more DVDs these days than anything else. One of the few truly Depression-proof businesses I can think of."

Surica chuckled. "So what do we do with Officer Moon, here?" Apparently she could read nametags as well as I could. *And* she was pretty.

I knew the guy was second generation Korean and a damned good cop. He'd come along shooting with Anton and me a few times and I'd tried the kimchee that his wife had sent with him for lunch. Sauerkraut is sauerkraut, I'm afraid, no matter how you try to dress it up. I've never really understood how people can stand the stuff. But it was worth a try. It usually is. I reached into my coat pocket for another card.

"Hey there, Moon." I spoke directly to the officer, looked him in the eye, and he came back to life almost like some kid's electronic toy.

"J Gifford. Nice to see you. What the hell have you been up to, man?"

"Nothing much, lately. My detective business has been pretty slow—you know what the economy is like these days—so I had to take a part-time job as an Immigration and Customs Enforcement agent. Here's my I.D." I showed him my plain old business card and *pushed*. "You're instructed to turn this suspicious individual over to my custody immediately."

He brightened. "Happy to do it, J, if it means I can get back to work."

I nodded and smiled. "It sure does. And Moon?"

"Yeah?" He'd gotten up, but he turned back.

"This is a national security matter that we're involved in, here." I lowered the tone of my voice. "You can forget that any of it ever happened."

"Okay, I will. Nice seeing you, J." And with that, Moon walked away.

○

"What happened back there?" Surica finally let go once we got back into the car. She'd been steady as a rock, but was shaking all over now.

"What part of what happened?" I asked. We stopped at a light and I took both her hands in one of mine, trying to catch her eye. I was worried.

"Why couldn't I control those two men, J?" It pleased me to hear her use what passes as my first name. "What did you do that was different?"

The light changed and we were off again. "It's probably because they were already under control. I was able to break it because of familiarity. I know that cop Moon personally and I've known at least a hundred of that poor security gink. Somebody had issued them their marching orders. Give you three guesses who, and the first two don't count."

She looked puzzled. "Then why make them?"

"It's just an expression, kiddo. Romanian has no silly idioms of its own? But you were right about one thing. In the state they were in, those two would have hauled you away and handed you over to the Warden."

"You would have come after me," she said, "and he would have us both."

"Something like that. You'd make a hell of a trophy. He's probably been mad as hell for twenty years, since he lost you back in 1989." I turned off the main drag and a few blocks up the feeder that led to the street I live on. "Although I can't imagine what he'd want with me."

She grinned back at me. It was a nice thing to see. "Perhaps he is bisexual. Or simply gay, since he never did anything with me in that way."

"That you remember." Turning into the alley behind the house, I said it before I could stop myself. Stupid, really. Between the sunshade and the headliner I pressed a button on the device clipped there.

The garage door opened and I drove inside. It closed behind us with a slam. I planned to lock it down firmly before we went into the house.

A long pause, then: "That's something to think about—that I remember. I was that man's prisoner for forty-five years. He could have done anything to me and made me forget it afterward, couldn't he? The fact it's never occurred to me before this isn't a good sign, is it?"

"Sorry, kid," I said, and I genuinely was. I stroked her hair.

"No," she shook her head. "Truth, however terrible, is a value in itself."

"Who said that?" It was a solid, quotable quote.

"I did." Squeezing my arm with both hands, she laid her head on my shoulder.

Brains are an aphrodisiac.

We didn't make it to the bedroom.

22: AN EVENING AT HOME

"Know that Allah is with those who guard
against evil."—The Quran

My friend Moe called me that evening, to confirm that I'd sent the young mall security guard to him. He was more than happy to give the kid a chance and, given a little training, even let him carry a gun. The guy figured that he still owed me for his tall, blond, slender, pretty American wife and the fifty or sixty kids they'd generated so far.

We always had the same discussion. That and the one about how I shouldn't get my pornography from the Internet. But the truth is, I've never been willing to pay for anything like that, and the only thing I'd obtained for Moe was his freedom. That he'd used it better than most individuals would have—to pursue his heart's desire, instead of that of his mother and father, sulking back at the family homestead in old Mumbai—was entirely his own accomplishment, and I told him so.

Again.

Thanks to her former keeper, Surica and I had pretty much missed our lunch. I'd be thinking about miso until I had a chance at another bowl. So I called out for pizza—no onion or garlic, of course—and we shared the girl who delivered it before going on to the main course. It sounds horrible, stated flatly like that, but it isn't, not at all. I gave the delivery girl a generous tip, but I always do that. The people who bring you food, especially when it's miserable outside, should be as well rewarded as possible. And, of course, she'd be a bit healthier, and live a little longer, for having delivered a pizza to us.

She was delicious, but it may have been the company.

Fiddlestring usually avoids events like that. He rejoined us for the pizza. He's nuts about Italian sausage, as who in their right mind isn't? It's also interesting the number of different drinks that go well with pizza: wine, beer, Coke. Even a mediocre wine or a lousy beer is better taken with pizza. About the only drink that doesn't is milk.

Yech.

I had about 1500 satellite and cable channels I could access, and big, flat screens all over the house, including the bathrooms. But as is often the case, there was nothing on TV that either of us found particularly interesting. We always found each other interesting, and were about to do something about that, right there in the living room, when the doorbell rang. I glanced down at my watch. It was just after nine.

Even at the best of times, there are certain individuals who think that the world would be a better, cleaner place without yours truly, so I take various precautions, especially after dark. Unholstering my .45 automatic, I held it behind the small of my back as I went to the inner door. As usual, Fiddlestring had "followed in front" of me as my backup.

Like the rear of the house, there's a big, glassed-in porch in front. They act like what you might call "solar airlocks," protecting me from being burned by sunlight whenever I have to answer the door. No problem with that at this time of the night and with that weather. Outside, waiting there on the porch step, stood Priscilla Varick, by herself.

I reholstered the Colt, opening the outer door for her.

"I hope it's not too late," she told me, as I followed her back to the living room. She'd left an umbrella and her topcoat on the porch to drip dry. She knew her way around well enough. We'd spent plenty of time together, me and the Varick family, over the years. I knew their house well, too. "Varick's got some sort of late-night regional task force meeting until about midnight, my two little birdies have flown from the nest again, and I have something important I need to say to you."

I gave her a suspicious eye. "And you can't wait to meet Surica."

"You're damned right I can't wait to meet Surica—hello, there! I'm Priscilla." She thrust a hand out. Surica took it, then embraced her. It was a very strange sight, and a sign that my life was already changing.

They sat down on the sofa. "I'm so happy to finally meet you. I've been worried about J for a long time. Are you also..." She reached up and delicately touched her own upper canine incisor. Surica smiled and nodded. "Good!" said Priscilla. "I have never believed in mixed marriages."

I laughed. So did Surica. What the hell had I ever done to deserve friends like the Varicks? "Can I get you a beer or something?" I asked.

"Tea, if you don't mind the trouble, hot tea." She shivered. I couldn't blame her. Outside, it had settled down to a slow, steady drizzle.

"I don't mind at all." I headed toward the kitchen. We'd never really had much of a summer this year, and it was shaping up to be a miserable excuse for an autumn. I filled the electric kettle and got it running. I pulled several different teas down from the cupboard and put them in a little porcelain bowl, set that and a matching cup on a reed tray, and by the time I'd accomplished that much, the kettle was boiling. Hot water in a little matching teapot beside the cup, a spoon on the side, milk, sugar, and lemon, and back out into the living room.

They sat sort of sideways, facing each other on the little sofa. Fiddlestring was sitting like a sphinx between them, purring his ass off.

Priscilla was telling Surica, "So in the middle of the movie he said to me, 'If you'd transfer to Von Mises, we could get married,' and that was his proposal. Tell the truth, aside from the fact that I knew he was the one the moment I saw him writing that citation, I was more than ready to get the hell out of Moscow on Boulder Creek. Von Mises Memorial may not be as sexy as the University of Colorado, but as colleges go, it's more practical—and much better screwed into reality."

Surica: "I'll keep that in mind, should I ever wish to go back to school." I don't believe she'd ever been to school, but she'd had tutors.

Excellent tutors.

Priscilla: "You really should, you know. You'd have all kinds of fun. Oh—except for the—but I guess you could sign up for night classes."

They both broke out in hysterical laughter. Night classes. Go figure what some people will find funny. It startled Fiddlestring. He got down off the sofa and left the room with an indignant twist of his tail.

Once we got settled, Priscilla with her tea, Surica with her wine, and me with a CooperSmith's Not Brown Ale, my best friend's wife got serious.

"I'm so glad Anton finally told you that we've known about you, J, almost from the beginning. We never even talked about it at home, to spare the kids too much strain keeping your secret. But they knew. How could they not know? Eventually we had to explain it to them as best we could—as well as we understood it, anyway—like the talk you have to have, sooner or later, about sex: 'Yes, Virginia, your Uncle J is a vampire, but he doesn't seem to bother anybody very much about it.'

"In point of fact, you don't look at all like a vampire, Gifford. You look a lot more like some basketball hero from a Norman Rockwell painting."

She turned to Surica. "Now you, you *do* look like a vampire—and I mean it only in the most complimentary way possible. Beautiful, slender, willowy, but amply built—like Joanne Kelly on *The Dresden Files.*"

That was a new one on me. I made a note to check it out. Hulu, probably.

"But I haven't gotten to the reason I came, J." I sat down in my favorite chair opposite the couch and Priscilla turned toward me. "I know you don't want thanks, but you have to understand something. I love my life.

I love my big, strong, all-too-silent husband. I love my son who's going to be just like him. And I love my daughter, whom I hope will be at least a little bit like me. I love the home we've all made together, and I love my work. I wasn't anywhere near ready to give them up, but it looked like I didn't have any choice in that matter."

Priscilla had been trained as an art historian. She did a little painting and sculpture herself, and even sold reasonably well in local shops. On birthdays and Christmases over a quarter century, she had given me enough art to decorate my house from one end to the other. If she couldn't restore a work of art herself, then she knew who could. But the main thing she was known for nationally was appraisals and authentications.

"It was easy to do, Priscilla. I gave you a little of my blood. I carry a virus—so does Surica—that eats cancer for breakfast and anything else that might ail the human constitution for lunch and dinner."

"A virus," Priscilla said thoughtfully. "I had no idea."

"I'd be happy to do it again, for anyone in your family and a couple or three other folks I know. But you must never tell anybody about it, or somebody might try to catch us and drain us—we don't have enough blood, between us, to save the world—or maybe just dissect us for the CDC. They won't succeed, of course, but a lot of people will have to die in the attempt, almost certainly including us."

She nodded solemn understanding.

"By the way," I said, "There's still some pizza if anybody's interested."

Fiddlestring stuck his head around the corner and said, "Miao?"

And that's when a man with a gun in his hand came through the door.

23: SOMETHING WICKED

"Nature has no principles. She makes no distinction
between good and evil."—Anatole France

The gun, being held between thumb and forefinger like a dead rat, was Anton's .40 caliber Glock M22, dripping water onto my hardwood floor.

So, for that matter, was Anton. The right side of his topcoat, the outside of his right pants leg, and his right shoe were wet and muddy. Oddly, his other side appeared to be dry. Anton was the old-fashioned kind of gentleman who suppresses his natural tendency toward profanity in the presence of ladies. I could see the strain of it now, in his face.

"Ever have one of those days?" he asked the room. "I had just gotten out of the car in front of the house, here, congratulating myself that my task force meeting had broken up early, when my foot slipped on something slick, and down I went. Luckily I carry my cell phone on the left side. It would be considerably harder to get dried out."

While Priscilla and Surica relieved Anton of his sodden topcoat—as I recalled, he didn't like wearing a suit jacket under it and had likely left it at his office—removed whatever he'd been carrying in his pockets, and spread the coat over a couple of plastic-coated metal chairs to dry, I went to my office for a gun cleaning kit I keep in a gym bag in the lower right-hand drawer of my desk where a fictional hardboiled detective is supposed to keep his traditional bottle of Bushmill's.

I kept mine in the kitchen, only it was Cuervo.

Opening the bag, I spread a couple of car mechanic's red rags on the breakfast counter where Anton's personal effects—badge flipper, wallet, gloves, two sets of keys, cell phone, and small notebook—were beginning to pile up, and extended an open hand for his waterlogged *pistola*.

"I'll do it," he growled. By now he was out of his wet shirt and trousers, his unmentionables, as well, and was wearing one of several bathrobes I never wear, myself. He took a pair of cased bifocals out of one of the pockets, perched them on his nose, and sat down on a stool.

Actually, it was good therapy for Anton's elevated blood pressure. For some reason there are few things in life more relaxing (petting a cat is one of them) than disassembling a personal firearm, cleaning it thoroughly, and putting it back together again. Maybe it has something to do with restoring some peace and order to one small corner of the universe.

Pressing a small rectangular button at the rear trigger guard root on the left side of the piece, Anton pulled the plastic box magazine from the underside of the handle. Some older Glocks don't drop their magazines automatically when you press the catch button, and Anton's was one of those. With fifteen rounds in the magazine—seventeen if you happen to be shooting nine millimeter—it may not be all that important.

"Shit!" Apparently Anton had forgotten about the ladies present. I would have, too. When the magazine had come out of the weapon, it had more or less poured water onto the red rags. Maybe a tablespoon full. He added, "I guess when I do a job, I make a point of doing it thoroughly!"

I laughed and got out some more red rags.

Anton pulled the slide back, and one of the .40 caliber Winchester "SilverTip" cartridges he used fell out of the ejection port onto the rags. They're not silver, but lead, with highly-polished cupronickel or aluminum jackets, depending on the caliber and age. These were the former.

I started unloading the magazine, pushing on the back end of each cartridge (for some reason known as the "head") with my thumb, and letting them fall onto another red rag. Unless Anton requested otherwise, I'd let him disassemble the magazine and dry it. It isn't complicated. Two spare magazines he carried on the offside had been perfectly dry. I didn't bother with them. If it ain't wet, don't dry it.

I rolled the cartridges around on the rag, drying them off. My guess was that, in spite of normal procedure in ordinary times, with ammunition as scarce as it was right now, Anton would want to use them again, as backups, if not for anything else. It was almost certainly an acceptable practice. The bullets were sealed into the case mouths with some kind of stickum, and the whole assembly had a shelf life of about a million years. Me, I'd shot .45 ammunition—and it wasn't that long ago—that had been manufactured during the First World War.

Not a misfire in the entire lot of a thousand rounds.

Meanwhile, Anton pointed the empty pistol in the safe direction of one of my herb planters (just in case) and pulled the trigger, which produced a noisy metal and plastic clank. Believe it or not, that was part of the official disassembly process. Then he held it in an odd grip that let him retract the slide about an eighth of an inch against the pressure of a powerful recoil spring, while he pulled down on a couple of little serrated nubs above the trigger guard, both sides of the pistol.

This released the slide to be pushed forward off the frame. I knew from experience that the polymer frame (for which read some kind of plastic) remaining in his right hand felt even lighter than balsa wood, not at all right, my every instinct told me, for a powerful high pressure cartridge like the .40. But my instincts were wrong. I also knew that the damned stuff was stronger, tougher, and would last much longer, than any equivalent part fabricated from steel. I've been told they have a specimen in Austria, where Glocks are made, that has been fired by some kind of automated machinery hundreds of thousands of times.

By contrast, a government model .45 is documented to be good for only 5000 rounds before it's supposed to be retired. Mine has gone at least four times further than that, but I keep an eye on it and baby it.

Still, plastic?

Where the Glock's frame was made of plastic, containing only a few small parts made of steel, the Glock's slide, easily comprising more than two thirds of the pistol's unloaded weight, was all steel, with no artificial additives of any kind. So much for being undetectable at airports.

Holding the slide upside-down in his left palm, Anton removed the captive recoil spring assembly—which was pretty wet—and then the barrel, and that was it. The whole pistol had now been broken down for inspection and cleaning into only five parts: magazine; frame; recoil assembly; slide; and barrel. Taking it further was properly work for a gunsmith.

Now it was time for toothbrushes (arguably one of the most useful multipurpose artifacts ever invented), round brushes for the bore and chamber, and one of those tiny brushes they sometimes pack with coffee makers. You can accumulate a lot of those if you live as long as I have.

Soon, a heady aroma from my youth, that of Hoppe's Number Nine bore cleaning solvent (I've often thought they ought to make an aftershave or men's cologne) was drifting through the house. Surica and Priscilla, both of whom knew their way around guns, pitched in with Q-Tips and a hair dryer. A drop or two of Tri-Flow, a lubricant allegedly containing microscopic little beads of Teflon, and we were finished.

Anton reassembled the Glock—he was the only one of us who had handled it; the rest of us had been drinking, and I draw the line just before a single beer—and laid it atop the counter. His Uncle Mike's holster was constructed of ballistic nylon and would dry out readily enough.

O

Anton accepted a drink—I do keep a little whiskey around, Jameson's—and leaned back on the living room sofa, stretching his long legs. I'd built a little fire in the tiny fireplace, and suddenly the cold and damp outside didn't seem to matter quite so much any more.

Cave people had probably discovered that 30,000 years ago, but it's always nice to reaffirm it. Of course they didn't have whiskey or tequila.

Poor cave people.

Without being asked, Priscilla had gone into the kitchen and prepared some food for a rainy evening: tomato soup, grilled cheese sandwiches. She knew where everything was. Canned Campbell's in the cupboard, mixed with water in a bowl, a dash of Lea and Perrins, heat in the microwave, add about the amount of half and half you'd add to coffee.

The sandwiches she produced were every bit as simple: bread (I like the kind with bits of nuts baked into it), American cheese, very thinly-sliced tomatoes, butter, hot griddle. Surica watched the whole process in fascination, never before acquainted with the concept of "comfort food." Given what I knew about her parents, I didn't wonder why.

We ate and drank for a little while, not saying much, watching the fire.

Then: "Nobody asked me about the meeting, the task force." Anton snagged another half sandwich from the plate—Priscilla cuts them from corner to corner, like my mom did—and sat back again, sipping whiskey.

The women didn't say anything. A look on Priscilla's face told me she thought that something was up. I said, "I wasn't going to ask you. I thought that kind of thing is secret. Homeland Security and all that."

"Not DHS this time," said Anton, "FBI. They came, along with cops from several different states, most of them southern. CBI was there, too."

Colorado Bureau of Investigation. By no means number one on my hit parade for competence or freedom from political influence. I didn't say so. Anton knew my opinion on the subject and to a certain extent even shared it. But he had to work with these people, and I didn't. All of a sudden, I was wondering why we were talking about this.

"So how come we're talking about this, all of a sudden?" I asked.

Anton sat up and put his glass down on the coffee table. "Because the task force concerns what they believe is an interstate serial killer. Given the nature of the killings, I thought you might have some insights."

He took in a huge breath of air and let it out. "Also, owing to peculiar circumstances, I have to do something I don't want to do, Giff. I have to ask Surica where she was the week before she got here."

24: SUSPICION

"The function of wisdom is to discriminate between good and evil."—Marcus Tullius Cicero

*N*obody cried "Anton!"

Priscilla bowed her head and put a hand over her eyes.

Surica sat serenely where she was, next to me, looking at the fire.

"A few days ago," Anton told us, "the mutilated body of a young groundskeeper was discovered in a public restroom in a park or county fairground in Leoti, Kansas. His throat been torn open and he had bled out completely. Or he had *been* bled out. In any case the stuff was everywhere. Absolutely the worst crime scene photos I ever had to look at."

I'd just told him that vampires don't need a lot of blood to get along.

"Something about that killing triggered fresh looks into similar deaths across the country. Our subject apparently likes dumpsters, and the body of an elderly dockyard security guard was found in one at the seaport of Charleston, South Carolina. The victim had been bled out completely, and his revolver was found nearby with all six chambers fired."

"You'd think he'd have taken the gun with him," I said.

Anton nodded. "You'd think. No bullets were recovered from the scene."

"As if the killer *did* take those with him," said Priscilla.

"As if," her husband agreed. "In Wichita, they found a dog in a dumpster, complete with collar, leash, and license tags that told them who its owner was. No one had seen her in a day or two. A broader search led the police to the body of a college coed in the basement of an abandoned downtown motel. Her dog's neck had been broken like a chicken's, and the girl had been bitten for her blood twice in twelve hours."

Interesting, I thought. "Had she been sexually assaulted?"

He shook his head. "The report was specific. No sign of it."

"Interesting," I said it aloud that time.

Anton said, "Apparently our perp departed from his M.O. in Tulsa."

I said, "Provided that's what it was, an M.O. Disposing of the bodies after he had fed on them may just have been governed by convenience. That's the very thing that dumpsters are designed for, right?"

"This is true," Surica agreed. "I freely confess that I preyed on German soldiers—they were my enemies, after all. I had shot them out of the skies with a song in my heart, and bombed and strafed them on the ground, before I lost my little airplane. Retreating from France after I left J there. I fed on their stragglers and, to the best of my recollection, got rid of the bodies in no single particular way."

Anton looked at Surica with an odd expression on his face, as if seeing her for the first time. Oddly, Priscilla was actually smiling. At the very bottom line, women can teach men a great deal about being fierce.

Surica touched him on the arm. "Yes, Detective Varick," she told him, "I am a vampire. But, exactly like J, here, over the years I have learned to be a moral vampire. At least as moral as I can be, in the circumstances."

"You have a point," he said. "About getting rid of the bodies. They found the one in Oklahoma half floating in the Arkansas River. It would have washed all the way down to the Mississippi if it hadn't hit a snag. That's when they decided to organize this federal task force and—"

"Let me guess," I interrupted. "They broadened their search criteria to take in the Arkansas River body and came up with...what?"

"A missing waitress in a culvert under a highway near one of those big truck stops outside of Atlanta. Throat torn out, no sign of sexual assault."

I said, "Almost as if the murderer were impotent." It was fairly common to kill out of sheer rage at not being able to do anything else.

"Or a woman," said Surica.

Anton nodded, "Or a woman."

Which brought us back around, full circle.

"They're still arguing about a body they found in a fleabag hotel in Memphis. Very, very messy, but the throat was cut, not bitten. A knife with two different blood types, one of them anomalous and unreadable for some technical reason. Interstate truck driver who'd dropped a container at a distribution center that day. Some witnesses say he wasn't alone. Multiple stab wounds, each of them potentially fatal."

"And no consistent description of the other person," I guessed.

"The oddest thing is that, while the anomalous blood evidence is consistent with traces discovered in the other killings we've been talking about—they think the murderer was shot at contact range by the dock watchman; the whole front of his uniform was covered with blood, not his own—the Memphis victim's blood is a DNA match for fingernail scrapings linked with an altogether different series of killings: truckstop prostitutes, three dozen over the last twenty years."

I raised my eyebrows. "Serial killer meets serial killer?"

He nodded. "That's what it looks like."

"Why does this news fail to fill me with rapture?" I asked.

"What sparked the task force meeting tonight was the discovery of more bodies—eleven of them—in Colorado Springs yesterday in a bombed-out shopping mall. They'd been dead for around four days. Each and every one of them, six males and five females, had their throats torn out in the way that we've come to expect. Nothing stolen. They haven't found any physical evidence, blood or skin parings, that it was the perp we're interested in, but with help from the DHS, they're keeping a lid on it until they've exhausted what forensics they do have."

Perfect: an entire federal agency dedicated to thwarting the free press and nullifying the First Amendment—or maybe just preventing a run on the country's precious and dwindling supplies of garlic. Still, I could imagine the joy with which the authorities and city fathers looked forward to announcing a serial killer who appeared to be a vampire.

I saw the pattern, and, of course, Anton—and his task force—would have, too. No matter what order the bodies had been discovered in, they mapped out an only slightly squiggly line from an east coast seaport straight to the state we lived in. According to Rand McNally it was 106 miles from Colorado Springs to New Prospect. Anton would be a fool not to be interested in when Surica got here and how she'd come.

It took me a surprisingly short time to come to a decision, and I was confident it was the big head making it, not the little head. I've probably seen five hundred XY types completely taken in by women they thought loved them. Men are idiots that way, but it's how evolution has designed them. Their job is to spread it around as far and wide as possible. It's the women who are the conservators of the human gene pool.

Of course I realized that I could be the five hundred and first idiot, that I could be completely wrong about Surica. It wouldn't make me the first fool for love in human history. I'd loved her—mostly from afar—for sixty-five years, ever since that wine cellar in France. The person I'd constructed in my imagination since then, out of little scraps of memory and lingering traces of ecstasy, could be someone altogether different from the person she actually was then, or the person sitting beside me on the sofa tonight. But she was right here, right now, and I believed, both in my mind and heart, I knew her.

And although neither of us had said a word so far about anything more lasting than a kiss at twilight, mentally, morally—yes, and emotionally—I'd thrown in with Surica Fieraru, as the cowboys say, for good. Sometimes an individual has no choice but to decide where his loyalties lie, well in advance of any useful information about how wise that decision may be. I wanted to get laid on a regular basis, that much is true. But I also wanted a partner. I was tired of living life alone, and it made me absurdly happy just to look at Surica's face.

Fiddlestring seconded the motion, crossing the rug and hopping into Surica's lap. She was ours and no matter what, we'd stick up for her.

Or perhaps a better choice of phrase was called for.

"Surica is a vampire," I told Anton. I reached over scratched the cat behind the ears. "Just like me. And just like me, she isn't a murderer."

He turned to me, his face lined with pain. "I don't think she is, either, Giff. I like her. My kids like her. Priscilla likes her. She's already as good as family. But I'm a policeman, and I'm obligated to ask."

I opened my mouth—to say what, I don't know.

Surica said, "Of course he is, my love. Of course you are, dear Anton." She composed herself on the sofa, giving the cat a pat or two. "I am one of these illegal aliens that everybody seems so concerned about. I arrived in North America at Halifax, Nova Scotia, in the hold of a Lithuanian cargo vessel. I had bribed an officer to let me do so. I had also purchased many false identification documents before I left Europe."

Anton ran a hand over his face and listened.

"I came across to Halifax myself," I said, "in May of 1945 after the end of the war in Europe. And on a Lithuanian ship." I looked directly at Surica. "I don't suppose any of this is a coincidence, is it?"

"It is not," Surica answered. "I was following you, in a way. Of course the trail had grown as cold as can be imagined, and yet it is not so cold for someone who can ask questions that *must* be answered. You were new to this life, then. And yet you were unwilling to kill in order to feed. I was able to follow your path from France up to the Baltic, going from one family legend and nightmarish memory to the next."

"Sounds like we could use you downtown," Anton told her, trying to smile.

"It was difficult," she said, "not only because I longed to find J—perhaps he has told you of my confinement by the Communists in Romania—but because I, too, was being followed. I think it possible that this follower, the Warden, Deabru, as he is known in the most ancient of European languages, may be the serial killer that you seek."

Of course the same thing had occurred to all of us.

25: THE GOLD STANDARD

"Goodness alone is never enough. A hard cold wisdom is required, too, for goodness to accomplish good. Goodness without wisdom invariably accomplishes evil."—Robert A. Heinlein

"Having driven a rented car by night from Halifax, resting during the day, I crossed the United States border on foot and by canoe, in the vicinity of Magnetic Lake, Minnesota, somewhere near County Road 12."

Cross-country travel is difficult if you're a vampire, but no more so than it was in decades past for black people whose situation I often thought about back in the 1950s. I agreed with Rex Stout's Nero Wolfe that if I had been born black, by then I'd have been in jail or dead.

Surica continued. "That country is cold, let me tell you, even in summer. The insects are terrible, and about two thirds of it is open water. From where I crossed, I hitchhiked to the little town of Ely. My American passport reads "Sophie Freelander," which I felt was appropriate, a real person who was born in Hibbing, in 1984, and died, unfortunately, at the tragic age of eighteen days. The birth date made me twenty-five years old, somewhat less than one tenth of my actual age."

Never able to resist a straight-line, I stifled a clownish urge to say she didn't look a day over a hundred. Truth was, she didn't even look twenty-five.

"Here is the silliest part of the story. At least it seems silly, now. I don't know whether because of what I am or what I went through after the war, I am able to place myself in a state of rest whenever I wish, consuming little oxygen and no food or water—or blood—for days at a time. From Ely, I drove a rented car to Duluth, where I had myself shipped by air in a sturdy wood box to a warehouse in Cheyenne, Wyoming."

That got everyone's attention. Priscilla, with a mother's concern, wanted to know if the box had been padded on the inside or had air holes drilled in it. Yes to the former, no to the latter. Anton wanted to know how she'd nailed herself in. She'd done it from the inside with a staple gun, she explained, called for pickup by cell phone from inside the crate, and nodded off to sleep. Once again, I nobly suppressed an almost irresistible urge to ask about frequent flyer miles.

"When I arrived at the warehouse in Wyoming, the alarm in my telephone awoke me. I broke out of the crate, found a place in the warehouse to change into the dress I wore to meet J in, and here I am."

She leaned toward Anton and gave him a humorously serious glare. "I have the invoice and other documents if you would care to see them, Detective."

"That I would," he glared back for an instant and then grinned. "As soon as possible. And thanks. You've taken a great weight off my shoulders."

"I am so sorry to have put it there to begin with. As I said, it is no coincidence if the Warden is headed this way. He is following me."

"Which means," I said, "that some preparations are called for."

Varick and his wife nodded.

○

"Mr. Gifford? I'm Jessica Lake."

The first of those preparations arrived bright and early the next morning on my front porch steps with an oversized sketchpad under one arm, and a laptop case swinging from the other hand. She couldn't extend a hand, so I held the door, beckoning her into the vampire's lair.

"Thank you. I work for Priscilla Varick. She sent me."

"I know. Call me J. I just got off the phone with Priscilla. You work for her husband Anton sometimes, too." New Prospect was too small a town for somebody of Jessica's talents to be on the city payroll full time. I took her jacket and placed it on a hook. It was beaded with drizzle. The "bright" part of that "bright and early" was only an expression.

Jessica ("Call me Jess.") was young, early twenties at a guess, not very tall, with pale, Celtic skin which went perfectly with the Irish sunshine coming down outside, and a shock of thick red hair, not quite shoulder length. A pair of wire-rimmed glasses perched on her nose. She wore jeans, sandals, and a man's light blue denim work shirt.

I introduced her to Surica, who was sitting on the living room floor with Fiddlestring in her lap, mentally preparing, I supposed, for what we both reckoned was going to be something of an ordeal. Jess plonked down beside her, opened up and booted her little computer. Instead of a mouse, she used an electronic drawing pad of some kind, the same width and depth as her computer, and a matching electronic stylus.

Apparently, though, she'd decided to start with paper and pencil. She cradled a big tablet in the crook of one arm and looked up at Surica.

"Ready to begin? Great. I take it that we're dealing with a man, right?"

Surica nodded. I could see this was already costing her something.

"Do you know his name? I find that sometimes helps me get the personality."

Surica began, but had to clear her throat and start again. I could see her hands shaking, but my chair was too far away to do anything constructive about it without being awkward. "Deabru," she answered. "When they spoke of him they called him Deabru—also known as the Warden."

Jess didn't bat an eye at that, where many another might have. "Deabru," she rolled the name around on her tongue. "Isn't that Basque?"

Surica and I both blinked. She nodded and said, "It means nightmare."

"And the shape of this Deabru's face: round, square, triangular, diamond...? Close your eyes. Imagine you're seeing him. Listen to him—"

"Round," Surica said suddenly. "Squarish or round. He looks young—early thirties, but he's older than that. His hair is dark but not black. He wears it close-cropped, not shaven or...what is the word, love?"

She'd looked to me. "Buzzed," I supplied.

"Yes, not buzzed." She went on, with only a little prompting from the artist, to describe the man of whom she'd been terrified for sixty years.

The man I was going to kill, if I could.

After a while, the women had achieved a degree of understanding, and I headed downstairs to the basement to make preparations of my own. I took a brand new box of .45 Automatic Colt Pistol ammunition with me, and a box of .38 Smith & Wesson Special. I'd bought both earlier that morning. They were not my usual brand, but had been chosen for the unusually wide and deep hollow points in their front ends.

For the next hour, I contented myself with hand-work that was almost as pleasant and satisfying as cleaning a gun. From a drawer in my loading bench, I took a pair of what's known as "hollow pointers," a relic of the bad old days when most factory bullets didn't come that way.

Never say "bullet" when what you mean is "cartridge." Understand that the "cartridge" is the whole thing that you put into the gun. The "bullet" is the part in front that gets pushed out of the barrel by the pressure of burning powder and, hopefully, finds its way to the badguy. What's left behind in a revolver like my .38, or gets kicked out the side of an autopistol like my .45, is the empty cartridge "case."

Learn that, and you won't sound like an east coast cop (that includes California), an idiot actor playing a cop on TV, or a TV newsie whose hairspray has soaked through his scalp and into his brain.

The device I was using is hand-held and very simple. Insert a cartridge into the back of a small, knurled cylinder, holding it there with your thumb. Insert the other part—a little chuck that holds a drill bit that you can adjust for depth—into a small hole in front and turn until it bottoms. Pull out the drill, drop the cartridge into your palm and you've got yourself a nice, deep, wide-mouthed hollow point.

Repeat until you've got blisters. When I was finally finished with the .45s, I did the .38s in a separate hollow pointing tool. Felt like forever.

Today I wasn't creating hollowpoints, just making them wider and deeper. From another drawer, I took a pair of latex gloves and put them on, necessary because the next thing I took from the drawer was a beat-up plastic baggie—it was so old and worn you almost couldn't see through it—full of hollow silver beads, each about three sixteenths of an inch in diameter, perfect for the hollow points I'd reshaped.

Why not use silver bullets? Because I didn't have the equipment to make them and I didn't have time. You can't just heat it up and pour it into a mold—when you see that in the movies, it's lead, not silver—you have to use a tiny centrifuge to drive it in at several gees. Also, silver shrinks a lot when it cools. A .45 mold produces .40s.

I didn't remember where I'd gotten those damned beads, maybe it was a thrift shop. Whatever they'd been strung on was long gone. Maybe wire, maybe string. There were at least a hundred of them, and I knew that they were pure silver—purish, anyway—because I'd burned the hell out of my fingers, accidentally establishing that. In 90 years, you collect lots and lots of oddities. I hated to think what my basement would look like in another 90 years. Love and marriage, horse and carriage, vampires and—pronounce it the English way, "gerridge"—sales.

I poured the beads into my case cleaner, a machine descended from a rock collector's tumbler, meant to remove tarnish, burned powder, and other things from the empty cartridge cases you're about to reload. Mine is old-fashioned; it's a small drum that really tumbles. The newer ones vibrate. They all use pulverized nutshells as a polishing medium.

While all that was happening on a shelf under the bench, I gave each hollow point a degreasing with alcohol and a Q-tip, and set the modified cartridges up in special wooden blocks meant to hold fifty at a time in nice neat rows of holes, and keep them that way. Then, on a plastic coffee-can lid, I extruded both halves of the components from a pair of epoxy tubes, and started mixing them with a toothpick. It was fairly cool in the basement and the stuff would take some time to set.

I put a single sticky drop in each hollowpoint.

I stopped the case tumbler, separated the now-shiny beads from the medium by pouring it all through a screen, and, being sure to use the gloves, carefully inserted a bead into each bullet, where it sank halfway into the epoxy. It was still liquid enough that some of the stuff would flow into the hollow beads, anchoring them firmly in place.

I now had a hundred vampire-killing cartridges, at least in theory.

I went upstairs to see what the enemy looked like.

26: FACIAL RECOGNITION

"It is a sin to believe evil of others, but it is seldom
a mistake."—H. L. Mencken

"Robert Downey Jr." Sandwich in hand, Quyen looked down over the shoulders of Surica and Jess at the portrait taking form on Jess's tablet. "Oh, hello, J. We brought a big box of gyros over if you're interested."

I was. Gyros, she'd said, famously known elsewhere as doner kebab, sometimes spelled donair or donar, kebap, or kebabi. Also known as yee-ros or yiros, shawarma or souvlaki. Some folks call them "donner kebab," but only in the Sierra Nevadas. Call 'em lamb-lathe sandwiches, I don't care. I love the stuff. I tossed a look of greeting at Surica. She looked up and smiled back at me—pretty bravely, I thought, given the memories being raked up. Silly as it may seem, my day was made.

"He looks more to me like Charles Bronson," Quinn argued. "The young Charles Bronson." The sandwiches had arrived with French fries and plastic-paper containers of soft drinks. I didn't know which soft drinks, because the cups were all printed with colorful and lavish praises for the Deschanes Brothers, "Finest Greek Food Since 2500 B.C."

Both Quyen and Quinn were completely correct, though. Jess's portrait of the fiend who haunted my lover's nightmares could have been morphed from photos of the two movie stars. The guy didn't look all that fiendish to me, but I suppose you probably had to have been there.

For forty-five years.

I said something about the morphing idea, over my shoulder, and grabbed a sandwich of my own from the box on the kitchen counter: pita stuffed with spicy lamb, tomato, onion, cucumber, and lettuce—you can keep my share of the olives—slathered in lovely yogurt sauce, and sprinkled with mild *feta*. I took a chance on one of the mystery drinks. Coke, the real thing. I have never been able to finish a Pepsi and I don't know why. The French fries were good: thin, crisp, still hot.

○

It would be corny to say that, in my job, I don't have to go out looking for trouble to get into, trouble comes looking for me. But in this case— I mean *in this case*—it was quite literally true. The epoxy in my bullets hadn't quite been set a full twenty-four hours when the doorbell rang. Raised lettering on the linen business card read:

Richard Francis Xopher

I turned the card over and read it out loud, pronouncing the X like a Z. There was nothing else printed or written on either side, just the name and a lot of expensive, empty space. Nodding to the man—closer, I thought, to Charles Bronson than Robert Downey—who had handed it to me, I let him in and we went back to the office together. My heart was pounding away like a machinegun, although I tried my best not to show it, but I knew he could hear it as well as I could, myself.

"You have quite a beautiful home, Mr. Gifford," he told me as I indicated a chair for him to sit in. To my ear, he didn't have any kind of accent I could detect, just literate midwestern American. I went around my desk and sat, as well. "Lots of glass—ultraviolet filtering, I assume—this place must be spectacularly cheerful in daylight."

"Too much darkness is depressing, even for one of us," I said.

"'One of us,'" he echoed my words. "I wonder what you think that means. Perhaps you'd prefer to be called by the name you were born with." He pronounced it. It was the first time I'd heard it in over sixty years, the first time I'd even thought of it in at least ten. Whoever that person had been, he wasn't me any more—or I wasn't him. Gifford, Illinois seemed like a long, long way away at the moment.

Without missing a beat, Xopher continued. "The school of 'Arts and Crafts'—sometimes referred to as 'American Craftsman.' You know, I was personally acquainted with both William Morris and John Ruskin. Their political ideals were fully as infantile as any other form of socialism, yet in the end, their followers brought to the world a new aesthetic."

Until the next trendy new designer came along, I thought.

He patted the chair arm. "I knew Gustav Stickley and his four brothers, as well. That items like this one, of furniture they made, would eventually sell in the market for hundreds of thousands of dollars is perfectly obscene; they themselves would have found it repulsive."

"You may be right, Mr. Xopher. I read somewhere that Barbra Streisand paid $363,000 for a Stickley sideboard, and I find her repulsive." Surica had said this was his first trip to America, as far as she knew. The Stickley brothers were from Wisconsin. I shrugged the contradiction off. "That's not a real Stickley, Mr. Xopher, but a good reproduction, handmade by a colleague of mine in Los Angeles named Mike Church. I did a little research for him in Denver a few years ago."

"And as such, a far better expression of Stickley's values than any overpriced original." He ran an appreciative hand over the plain cherry woodwork. "Clean designs. Quality homes and furnishings selling for what ordinary individuals could afford. 'Honest goods at honest prices,' as Iver Johnson once put it. I knew him, as well, and Martin Bye."

"The arms and cycles guy," I told him, wondering who the hell Martin Bye was. I'd often had the same thought, myself, about Stickley. Surica was listening from my study. Quinn and Quyen were in the kitchen with Priscilla, using their little laptop to look our visitor up, which is why I'd spoken his name aloud. Lacking our sense of hearing, they were listening electronically. I didn't know where Anton was. Prowling around outside somewhere like a big cat. "So what brings you here now, Mr. Xopher. Maybe something special I can do for you?"

He shook his head. He'd removed his hat and gloves, laying them on the broad chair arm. For some peculiar reason, this broke the spell, somehow, and it became easier to remember the bloody trail of mangled corpses this murderer had left sprawling across the country. "Indeed no, Mr. Gifford. Quite the contrary. I've come to do something for you."

I'd calmed down enough by now to give the man a good looking over. Richard Francis Xopher appeared young—in his early thirties, I'd have guessed—just as Surica and I did, for exactly the same reason. He was dressed extremely well in what I thought must have been Armani. What he'd paid for his shoes alone could have purchased every board foot of furniture—Stickley or not—and most of the artwork in my house.

Surica was terribly afraid of the man. I didn't need to hear her heart beating—although I could, and so could he—to appreciate that. I knew that right now she'd be clutching her little pistol, her palms sweaty on the hard rubber grip panels. I couldn't blame her. At his command, she'd suffered half a century in a cold, dark hole in the ground.

She'd warned me that the man was an intelligent, sophisticated being of almost irresistible charm—valuable survival adaptations for a vampire—and unmitigated evil. He'd surprised me, speaking my real name. I wondered how he'd react if I called him "Warden." Or Deabru.

Instead, I said, "You're going to do something for me?"

Xopher rose, took off his topcoat—we dressed amazingly alike: long coat, wide-brimmed hat. Only what he wore had come from Milan, Paris, New York, London, Tokyo, Shanghai and Dubai; mine was strictly from Wal-Mart—draped it over the other chair arm, and sat down again.

"Please permit me to speak plainly," he said. "There is a great deal I could do for you, Mr. Gifford. Of course it's difficult to know absolutely, but I am very likely the wealthiest individual person in existence. I am remarkably powerful, in more manners of speaking than just one. And I am most certainly the oldest. I am very, very old, indeed."

Xopher had miscalculated. I knew that he wanted Surica, but if I accepted a bribe to give her to him, then who would I spend the money with? Anton and Quinn would have understood in an instant. Why didn't Xopher?

"And how old would that be, exactly?" I asked, knowing that whatever he was about to tell me was almost certainly going to be true. But it was still like talking to some spiritualist hootie who thought that he was the reincarnation of Cleopatra or Alexander the Great.

Xopher shrugged. "I cannot say how old, exactly, Mr. Gifford, for I was born long before men began to count the years. This much I can tell you: I don't merely *know* what happened to the Neanderthals," his voice fell to a throaty whisper. "I *am* what happened to the Neanderthals."

I heard a slight scuffing noise to my right. Surica was standing a bit stiffly in the doorway, the expression on her face impossible to read. The lady stood there quietly, not looking at me or at anything else in the room. Her attention was focused entirely on her former captor.

27: HIGH NOON AT DUSK

"The belief in a supernatural source of evil is not necessary; men alone are quite capable of every wickedness."—Joseph Conrad

Surica didn't speak a word.

"Ah, there you are, my dear," Xopher told her in a patronizing tone. "I was wondering whether I might get to see you this evening or if you would spend it lurking there in the other room. I would say that you look lovely, but I'm afraid I can't, in all truth. You appear wild, unkempt, undisciplined. Freedom isn't everything it's supposed to be, is it? It's fairly obvious it doesn't suit you particularly well."

He turned to me, his charm beginning to devolve into smarm. "I confess I'm unaccountably fond of the girl, as I gather you are, too, for all that she is flighty, unreliable, unfaithful—as you will eventually discover to your chagrin and regret—and simply not very bright."

I felt my fist tighten on the grip of my .45 under the desk. I turned to see Surica still motionless, as if her mind was lost in some other space or time. Something was very wrong. My Surica would have killed this asshole outright by now and left his carcass for the coyotes.

"But you have asked me why I'm here, and I rudely allowed myself to become distracted, in part, by this vision of pulchritude, and neglected to answer you. I am hunting, Mr. Gifford. I am on the hunt. I have for several centuries preyed upon other vampires. As many as I could ferret out. For perhaps a thousand years, I have been in the process of deliberately rendering each and every one of them quite thoroughly extinct."

"Right," I answered, keeping a grip on my .45. "You're a real humanitarian."

"I see no need to be insulting, Mr. Gifford. In any case, you misunderstand me. What do I care for your precious *Homo sapiens*? What am I saying—*sapiens*? Your species haven't even *begun* to think yet. They may, in fact, prove incapable of it, in the end. And with each and every passing year, their little lives flicker by me faster and faster, like those of mayflies, or the sparks rising and winking out over a campfire. Eventually, I will remember this dialogue—and you—only as one single fleeting moment among a billion others."

"Okay," I nodded as if it all made sense. "I always wondered why I'd never met another vampire. You're saying it's because you ate them all?"

He spread his hands. "Oh, no, I didn't *eat* them, Mr. Gifford. The mere idea of doing so makes me feel nauseated. Even you should know by now that a vampire cannot be nourished by another vampire's blood. For the purpose of nutrition, I prey on humans, just as you do."

"Even me?" I blinked. Not telling tales out of school, mind you, what Surica and I did in private often involved bloodletting, and it always seemed nourishing to me, in some sense of the word. "Well I hate to break it to you old pal, but we're humans, too, you, me, Surica. We just happen to be carrying around a symbiotic virus in our blood."

He snorted. "I have heard this theory. Mere Pasteurist propaganda, and I choose not to believe it. At the least, *old pal*, we are a new species. Spiritually, I believe us to be elevated beings. I hunt down and kill my fellow vampires for one solitary simple reason: self- preservation."

"How's that?" I'd heard murderers try to justify themselves before, a dozen or more of them on the radio or TV from the White House.

"Consider Vlad Tepes as a chief example, the most notorious of our kind. I detested the little dragon—Dracula, as he styled himself—for his cheap, flashy theatricality, which always threatened to expose others."

"Including you." I offered.

"*Especially me*," he agreed. "It was at a dinner party, in a room with curtained windows that opened out upon his famous killing field. Ten thousand died that night as we dined upon his other guests. Then I greatly enjoyed killing him, as well, by impaling him on one of his own wooden posts. That, alone, wouldn't have killed him, of course. So I watched and listened to his cowardly screaming, as the sunrise took him."

I shook my head. "There really was a Dracula, and you killed the guy."

"One of your own United States Presidents was a vampire, you know. I had planned to kill him, too, but someone else got to him before I did."

"Which president was that?"

"Think it through, Mr. Gifford, it's obvious enough. Think it through."

The trouble was there were too many likely candidates.

"In the last few years, I have pursued your inamorata slowly as she searched, so that she would lead me to you. It is possible, Mr. Gifford, that you are the last vampire in North America. When I am through with you—and with her—my work on this continent will be done."

"But first..." I said.

"But first you must tell me what I want to know. What you know I want to know. It will be greatly to your benefit if you choose to cooperate."

"What if I told you I have no idea what you're talking about?"

"Then obviously, you would not benefit. I won't try to fool you: the information you have is very important. One way or another, it will figure in the lives or deaths of millions, perhaps tens of millions. Please don't insult both of us, denying what we both know is true."

The trouble was, I *had* no idea what he was talking about.

"Here," he said. "I will begin the process, showing you something that I know. And then you will tell me all the rest of it." He arose from the chair. I shoved my autopistol into my waistband and rose with him.

He approached Surica where she still stood beside the desk, almost like a statue, and extended his right hand, palm up. She gave him her left hand and he took it gently. Then he reached into a pants pocket, pulled out a large folding knife, and opened it with the touch of a button.

Instinctively, my hand started for my gun.

"Do not be alarmed, Mr. Gifford, it is only a demonstration of a scientific nature. I mean her no harm." He pricked her index finger with the tip of the blade, turned her hand over, and let a drop fall on the polished hardwood floor at their feet. "Now is your turn," he said.

Curious, I stepped around the desk, and when he gestured for it, offered him my own hand. He pricked my finger, too, and let the drop of blood fall into Surica's there on the floor. I had no idea what to expect.

Suddenly, the surface of the tiny two-drop pool became agitated, as if it were just about to boil. Within the space of mere seconds, something began to grow, a tiny form, from zygote to the miniature form of an adult human being, twisted and writhing with agony, in only a few horrible seconds. I thought I heard a tiny scream before Xopher stopped the process by stamping it into a messy stain on the hardwood floor.

Horrified, I still had no idea what it meant.

"Tell me what I want to know. I will be quick," Xopher demanded. "Otherwise she will die as slowly and horribly as I can manage, while you are forced to watch, then you will die slowly and horribly, as well."

For the first time in my life, I felt my fangs suddenly erupt from my gums as I leaped for Xopher's throat. But the older man was much too fast for me. He easily sidestepped my lunge and knocked me to the floor.

"Stay there!" Xopher commanded. I felt my muscles tense, and I knew that he was trying to push me, So, as I stood up, I pushed back, hard.

"Sit down over there and shut up!" I told him. His body jerked around in the direction of the chair, but he stopped suddenly, and grinned.

"A very creditable attempt, Mr. Gifford. Quite surprising, really." He turned to Surica. "All right, there's no point. Finish him."

Surica turned toward me and raised her right hand. Her Beretta had been hidden all this time within the folds of her skirt. Trembling with the effort to resist, she leveled the weapon on me, and with tears streaming down her face, pulled the trigger. I felt a hot slap at my left shoulder, a handspan from my heart, but kept my feet under me.

"Forgive her," Xopher said smugly. "She was my personal property for—"

Surica's gun went off again, but this time it was aimed at Xopher's face. The little bullet took him just to the left of his nose. She fired five more times and then the Beretta's slide locked back.

Xopher's face was a hideous ruin, and I doubt that he could see. He lunged for her, his clawlike fingers outstretched for her flesh, but the first big slug from my .45 knocked him off course. The next seven did for his chest what Surica's volley had done for his face. I'd saved the ninth in the chamber and swapped magazines as he came at me.

He never made it. Suddenly one of his knees exploded in a crimson cloud, and, as he shrieked, the other knee exploded as well. Jerking himself along the floor with his hands, he threw himself through the front window and, in a shower of broken glass, was gone into the night.

I turned. My shoulder had already stopped bleeding. Surica was sitting on the floor, drained, her skirt a colorful swirl all around her.

In the door to the hall stood Quinn, his .44 Magnum smoking in his hand. Quyen was right behind him with a little compact auto of some kind.

He grinned. "That's the way we do it in Jersey."

Only he said, "Joisey."

Suddenly, from the outside, we heard six more shots, then the gunning of a big, powerful engine and the squeal of tires. Surica was out the front door immediately, swapping .380 Beretta magazines as she went. I jumped out the broken window that Xopher had made his escape through.

Anton lay on his face in front of the house, halfway on the cement driveway, halfway on the rain-sodden lawn. I could see before I got to him that his right arm had been driven over and was crushed at the elbow.

His Glock lay in the middle of the drive, six feet from his hand.

28: DESPERATE MEASURES

"Evil is inevitable, but is also remediable."—Horace Mann

*P*riscilla got to her fallen husband before I did, throwing herself to her knees beside his body, patting ineffectually at his blood-soaked sleeve.

She was clearly afraid of injuring him more.

Surica and I reached his side a moment after that, squatting down. We shared a glance. Both of us could tell, from the unhealthy way he was breathing and the faint flutter we could both hear of his failing heartbeat, that there was a lot more wrong with him than an injured arm.

He had minutes left. The smell of death was already on him. I didn't want to turn him over or move him. Priscilla looked up, saw the way that Surica and I were regarding one another, and cried, "Yes, do it!"

"Even if—" I started.

"Even if!" Tears streamed down her face. "We'll live with it! You do!"

Surica saw me nod and was on her feet, running toward the house. I called after her, unnecessarily, to hurry, then turned my attention back to Anton. If his heart stopped beating, I would have to turn him over to keep him going. Not knowing the extent of his injuries, I desperately didn't want to move him. "Hang in there, help is on the way!"

Clearly, the silver beads had worked, or Xopher would just simply have walked away. I had no illusion he'd been finished off; I wouldn't have been. Yet I couldn't believe he still had this kind of murderous energy left in him. As I worked over Anton, Quinn and Quyen, behind me, were speculating that the virus might create a secondary circulatory system, stimulating arteries and veins to expand and contract—the latter, of course, already have one-way valves to help the process along—while the heart was being encouraged to repair itself.

Sometimes it's good to have distractions like that.

Before I could add my own two cents' worth to the seminar, Surica had returned with my kit. I took one of the large syringes I sometimes use instead of a Vacutainer to draw blood, plunged it by feel into my own carotid, letting it fill as quickly as it could. Barely able to find Anton's carotid by now, I injected him, but I didn't notice any immediate improvement, so I drew more blood from the other side of my neck.

As I turned, I noticed that Surica was doing the same thing to herself, probably on the time-tested principle that more is better. She shrugged and gave me a tiny, rueful grin, speaking in a voice so low Priscilla couldn't hear her as she injected her blood into our friend. "If he turns, we'll both be his sires. It'll be like he's our son."

Suddenly, Anton's heartbeat strengthened noticeably in power and consistency. He took a ragged breath, then another, very deep, and then groaned. Priscilla's eyes grew wide with hope. She put her teary face down on the concrete next to his and murmured to her husband quietly.

I got up on my knees, and then to my feet, giving Surica an unnecessary hand. "Is that how you feel about me, like I'm your little boy?"

She took it seriously. "No, my lovely man, not in the slightest. Sometimes it feels as if you sired me in that cellar, not the other way around. You awoke something in me that I had long thought was dead."

What can you say to that?

O

"Definitely *Homo heidelbergensis*," Quyen declared, peering at the big living room television screen. "Except for the nose, of course, and I always wondered about that, anyway. Reconstructors can only make guesses about soft tissue." She'd burned a DVD of her little computer's recording of my conversation with Deabru. Interview with the vampire. "He could be fifty thousand years old, maybe even older than that."

"Cleverly disguised, of course," Quinn added. "Gotta be theatrical prosthetics; I don't suppose plastic surgery works for you guys, does it?"

He was right, of course. I opened my mouth to say so, but Quyen spoke again before I could. "There it is all the same, for the trained eye to see. Heidelberg Man, big as life in the 21st century. They're currently believed to be the ancestors both of *Neanderthalensis* and us."

"Of course that could change tomorrow afternoon," Quinn shrugged. "It's all up in the air these days. The whole damn field has become extremely political, and Xopher could represent a third evolutionary branching. Fossilization is such a rare process there's no way to know."

"In any case, I think the fellow may be right," said Quyen. "He isn't human, not exactly, but a different species. I sort of expected that."

Fifty thousand years old. I raised my eyebrows. "How come?"

Looking down at her lap, she grinned, suddenly a little shy. "Well, I noticed right away that there weren't any rapes along his route from

Charleston to Colorado. It's just a guess, but I'd suggest that human females don't attract Mr. Xopher, any more than, say, female chimpanzees attract human males. They give off the wrong pheromones."

Her husband grinned. "I'm not so sure about that. I once knew this zookeeper—"

Quyen started to reply but it was her turn to be interrupted.

"I think I knew the same guy," Anton offered, "back when I was a rookie and working in the jail. Only with him, it was this Labrador retriever. Anybody care for another beer?" He started to get up. Priscilla pushed him back into the recliner and tucked an afghan in place.

That reminded me of another dog story, from the first *Terminator* movie, but I manfully repressed the urge to repeat it. I was still trying to absorb the idea that Xopher might be fifty thousand years old.

Maybe even older.

"You stay where you are," she told him, trying to be stern. "I remember how tired I was after J...well, you know. You'll need to rest."

The cops had come and gone by now. Alerted by reports of gun fire—.40 S&W is one hellaciously loud cartridge—they'd arrived to find a man with fresh blood all over his shirt nursing a sore back and elbow.

It helped that he was their Chief of Detectives.

"It's all very embarrassing," he'd said. "My wife Priscilla and I—you know the boys, Honey, Mike Blessing and Bill Koehler?—were visiting with our friends the Giffords, here." I nodded to both of the patrolmen, who knew me. "When the whole neighborhood, which is pretty quiet, normally, was rattled by what turned out to be repeated backfires coming from some kind of ancient flivver roaring down the street."

"A Model A Ford, I think." I was trying to be helpful.

Anton agreed, "That's right, a Model A Ford." But the man glared at me as if to say he could tell his own damned lies, thank you very much.

The cops both nodded with what they took for sudden understanding. I confess that I helped them just a little bit, pushing them gently to believe.

Anton sighed and shook his head. "Not knowing yet that the source was merely automotive, I went out to see what was happening, which is where I slipped on the wet pavement in the dark. I wrenched my back, bruised my elbow, bloodied my nose, and ruined a perfectly good shirt."

My friend had told his first vampire lie.

Next, he'd be claiming he had lupus.

The youngsters had believed him, of course, and had gone away with the warm satisfaction that comes only from learning that one's glorious leaders are all too human, and demonstrating, along the way, that a good pratfall will cover many a greater sin. When the front door finally closed behind them and their headlights swept the glistening street and disappeared, he spoke again as I turned from the door.

"Xopher will be back, as good as new, just like me. What do we do now?"

For a moment, an image of Neanderthal families flashed through my mind, huddled in their caves around a tiny fire, asking the same question.

Their answer, of course, had been, "Die."

29: THE SILVER STANDARD

"The only thing necessary for the triumph of evil is
for good men to do nothing."—Edmund Burke

*I*n addition to my two Colt handguns, I have a shotgun, as well. It's a 12 gauge "slide-operated" Model 870 Remington (for which read, "pump") with a short twenty-inch barrel, a long six-round magazine, and a pistol-gripped black plastic stock and forend. I bought it in a pawn shop because its menacing looks appealed to me—a shotgun *ought* to look menacing—and only found out later that it is almost perfectly worthless for shooting at claybirds or the real thing.

Anton had thought it was hilarious. He was another member of the Browning Superposed clan, only he favored 20 gauge for taking birds and their surrogates. The Remington is a fighting shotgun, nothing more.

But nothing less, either.

Ordinarily, since I don't own a rifle, I load the shotgun with shells that are either filled with quarter-inch "#4" buckshot pellets, or a single one-ounce solid "slug." At about .73 caliber, 437 grains' weight, and almost 1700 feet per second, slugs are the most potent weapons in the household arsenal, the nearest you can get to a good old-fashioned British elephant gun. It seems to work, too: I haven't seen a single old-fashioned British elephant since I bought the damn thing.

Or any married ones, either.

I didn't know how much time we had before another visit from the Warden—Richard Francis Xopher, as he called himself—or Deabru, a name that countless generations of paleolithic Europeans had probably only dared whisper. Certainly not enough. He'd be back just as soon as he had recovered enough for another fight—it had taken me a couple of months to grow a new pinky, but I wasn't going to make assumptions about the healing powers of a fifty-thousand-year-old vampire caveman who'd seen it all and done most of it twice, himself—and he'd be *pissed*.

I certainly would have been.

Anton had taken a few days off—they owed him, since he'd worked right through what had looked to be Priscilla's mortal illness—to help me solve the problem of dealing with an adversary (and when I say "dealing" I mean "killing") who had managed to survive others trying to kill him for at least fifty or a hundred thousand years so far. Emulating Scarlett O'Hara, Anton said he'd figure out what to do about his delicate condition—with regard to his job with the city—later.

Fifty or a hundred thousand years. I knew it. I believed it. But it was still difficult getting used to an idea like that. This guy had certainly seen wooly mammoths when they were still alive and well. He had probably even watched the giant critters being hunted and killed by my ancestors, as well as by Neanderthals. Cave bears, too. And dire wolves and saber-toothed tigers. Giant wooly rhinos with six-foot horns.

He wouldn't have seen any giant sloths, though, they were North American.

The next morning, after some perusal of the Internet and a couple of telephone calls, I asked Quinn to join Anton and me in what I hoped would be a brief expedition into Darkest Denver, with the object of securing what I thought would be needed to solve our little problem. We took my old Suburban, with its deeply tinted ultraviolet-proof windows.

I was about as well prepared as I could be—with my long coat, dark glasses, floppy-brimmed hat, and sun block—for whatever walking out into the deadly sunlight I might have to do in pursuit of my objective. What was truly weird was seeing Anton dressed the same way. We looked like a pair of aging fraternity brothers who had lost a bet.

The womenfolk—who would have been greatly annoyed at being called womenfolk: Surica, Priscilla, and Quyen—had stayed back at the house, attempting to prepare for the next onslaught. This was our fight, mine and Surica's, and I'd desperately wanted everybody else to go home. I felt more and more uneasy at having involved my friends—the only family I had in the world—in something that could get them killed.

"Surely you don't think Xopher's going to forget who shot his kneecaps off," Quyen had put it bluntly. "He'll come after us if you lose."

Her husband had spent the morning epoxying the rest of my silver beads into the front ends of half a box of .44 Magnum 240-grain hollowpoints.

"Aside from thanking you for your supreme vote of confidence, Mrs. Kowalski, I don't really know what else to tell you." She'd been totally right, of course. This bastard troglodyte had imprisoned my Surica for damn near half a century, and had tracked her since 1989. He wasn't ever going to forget somebody who had used his patellae for tiddly-winks.

Quyen hadn't shot the guy, but only because she hadn't gotten the chance. Quinn took up a lot of room in that doorway. She'd been right behind him—I'd seen her plainly enough myself—but by the time she got around her man-mountain spouse and lined up the sights of her Glock— a brand new .357 SIG—the Warden had escaped any further abuse.

Unless Anton had managed to connect as well, outside. He couldn't remember.

"Then kindly permit us to attend to the tactics here and you go get what you need down in Denver." Surica and Priscilla had ganged up on us, agreeing with Quyen wholeheartedly. The three of them were as well provided for, self-defensewise, as circumstances permitted. Priscilla had a well-worn Ruger Security Six .357 Magnum, Quyen had her Glock, and Surica had her Beretta. My .45 hadn't done that much more damage to Xopher than my girlfriend's silly little .380. The whole reason for this pilgrimage south was to obtain more effective ordnance.

So that's the way it had been.

O

One of my pet—though admittedly trivial—annoyances is people who insist on saying "joolery," rather than pronouncing it "jewel-ry." They drive me almost as crazy as the illiterates who pronounce it "nook-you-ler."

They certainly didn't make that mistake at Acme Precious Metals and Findings, a wholesale "jewel-ry" supplier located in Commerce City, an industrial suburb more or less buried in the northern part of Greater Denver, known best for its scenic—and highly aromatic—oil refinery. The young lady behind the counter was very bright and well-spoken.

"Yes," she said, "I think we have what you want. How much do you need?"

I smiled and told her, "That needs to be determined. We have to measure. Can you take us to the spool or bring the spool to us?" I don't know why, but in my sunproof get-up—if Anton and I struck the girl as a little strange, she was polite and didn't show it—I was feeling a lot like the shaky old man at the end of *2001: A Space Odyssey*.

All I needed was a cane.

Yeah, I know he didn't have a cane.

I pulled a partially loaded dummy shotgun shell out of my pocket. The girl took a step back, but Anton showed her his badge and assured her that everything was right as rain, whatever the hell that means. I regretted the necessity. A person should be able to buy whatever he wants for whatever purpose he wants, and not be hassled by the rabbit people.

She nodded gamely and came back, barely holding up a big spool of incredibly fine one hundred percent pure silver chain. I put on a pair of latex gloves—the girl had to be calmed down again; there must be something in the water of Commerce City that turns people into timid little field mice—and sort of drizzled enough of the stuff into the shell to fill up the polyethylene shot cup inside it. I pulled it back out again, and keeping my rubber-protected thumb and forefinger in place, measured the amount of chain that had fit inside the shell against a printed paper yardstick taped to the underside of the glass countertop.

At my inquiry, the girl told me the price. Quinn whistled. "Do you have any idea how expensive it's going to be, every time you pull the trigger?"

I think she decided that she hadn't heard that.

"Yeah, and every time I do, it's gonna make me madder until he's dead." I glanced at the girl again. Her eyes had gotten big. "Forget I said that," I told her, pushing her only a little bit. "This is purely theoretical."

Quinn and Anton didn't even notice what I'd done. I had the girl multiply the length by seven—the number of shells my shotgun holds; there wouldn't be time to reload—paid her in cash, and, once the chain had been properly measured, cut from the spool, and lay safely in its own zippered plastic baggie, took my gloves off and shook her hand.

If we'd been alone, I would have "bitten" her.

30: IF YOU WOULD HAVE PEACE...

"Evil is not something superhuman, it's something
less than human."—Agatha Christie

Getting home seemed to take forever.

It always makes me nervous when there's somebody else driving, and doubly so when they're driving my car. Unfortunately, I've never found a windshield glass that filtered the ultraviolet to my satisfaction, and we hadn't had much choice with regard to the business hours of Acme Precious Metals and Findings. So it was back to I-25, north to the middle off-ramp to New Prospect, and eventually the Suburban slid into my big garage beside the PT Cruiser as the heavy door swung down.

I hollered through the connecting door that we were home, not waiting for an answer. Instead of going into the house, I conducted my guests downstairs, the basement being accessible from the garage as well as the kitchen. That's where I keep my basic cartridge reloading setup. The room is cool, clean, and dry. I had painted over a pair of windows—a surprising number of individuals don't understand that reloading is perfectly legal—but had hung plenty of lights here and there.

Incandescents—I hate fluorescent light.

I can reload spent shells from my .45 and .38, but seldom do it much, preferring factory loads with bullets that do fancy tricks on impact. I reload shotgun shells whenever Anton and I go out to murder little clay disks, so he can laugh at me. I'm terrible at the sport. The way I have to dress in daylight may have something to do with that.

With Anton and Quinn watching me, I rummaged through a big plastic bin of fired shells until I found seven that matched. This practice is a bit less silly than it may appear. All other things—powder, shot, and primers—being equal, shells that are as identical as possible tend to shoot more or less identically, which means that you have an idea, having fired one, where the next slug or load of buckshot is headed.

The steps were relatively simple. I used a bench-mounted device—called a reloading press—designed to remanufacture pistol and rifle cartridges, rather than one dedicated strictly to reloading shotgun shells. They make those, too, but they always seem so flimsy and overcomplicated.

Screwing a machined cylinder called a "resizing die" into the top of the press, and snapping the proper shellholder into the "ram," the part that moves up and down, after some adjustment, I reshaped the seven cases (they expand when they're fired) at the same time removing the spent primers, the little part the firing pin hits to ignite the gunpowder.

Next, I used the machine to push new primers into the back ends of the cases. After that, a measured amount of smokeless gunpowder went into each shell, dispensed by a special little device screwed to the bench. I then installed a plastic "shot cup" in each shell to seal in the powder and hold whatever projectiles I intended to fire from the gun.

Now came the unusual and interesting part. Normally, I'd have used another dispenser, not unlike the one for powder, to pour lead shot of the desired size into the cases, or slipped in a slug by hand. This time, putting on another pair of gloves, I poured the silver chain out of the Ziploc bag and measured it into seven equal parts. I used a pair of tiny sidecutters on it, although the stuff was so fine and soft I could have used a butter knife, or a pair of kindergarten scissors. I then slithered a piece of the chain into each of the seven shells.

There followed a stage in which the crimp was started—which means I was closing up the front end of the shell, over the silver chain—and another that finished the crimp. And there they stood, seven shells that looked almost as good as if the factory had made them.

The whole process had taken less than half an hour.

As a final precaution, I loaded six of the shells into the Remington's tubular magazine and, shucking the forend back and forth (I added the seventh when there was room for it), made sure they fit the weapon and fed properly. This process had been highly recommended, among others, by a professional African hunter, guide, and author who'd watched one of his clients stomped flat and torn limb from torso by an elephant he'd managed to annoy but failed to kill when his rifle—the client's—jammed on ammunition that had been untried this way.

"All right, gents," I said, taking off the gloves and gathering up the freshly reloaded shotgun. "Let go upstairs and say hello to the ladies."

O

I once had a cartoon above my desk that showed one vulture telling another, "Patience, hell! I'm gonna kill something!" It's still around somewhere, yellowed and brittle. It pretty much summed up my attitude over the next week. I'm normally a fairly patient individual. It pays to be in my line of work—waiting in the rain at night in some dirty alley with only a dumpster to talk to—but it was much harder, this time.

In the first place, we had no idea where Xopher was holed up. It could have been in that dumpster I mentioned. It could have been in the Presidential Suite of New Prospect's answer to the Ritz. Some detective I was. Anton had put the word out to his men to be on the lookout for the guy— and he'd poked the multijurisdictional task force—although what he'd said beyond that, I had not the foggiest idea.

Some detective I was.

My greatest worry was that, having been on Red Alert since Xopher had shown up at the house, we'd grow lax and fall off our guard. I was morally certain our ancient enemy was counting on it. I wasn't certain how we could prevent it. Nobody can survive on an adrenaline rush forever.

Anton and Priscilla had more or less moved in for the duration, using a spare bedroom upstairs. They talked between themselves, not really arguing, about whether she should "go all the way" as he had. The Kowalskis had moved in, as well, into the study off my office, although they lost money every day they were away from the facilities in their own home. I promised myself I'd make it up to them somehow. I had an inkling, but I wasn't prepared to examine it too closely yet, myself.

Surica and I continued to live like honeymooners, the inclination heightened by the fact that each day—each hour—might be our last together.

Again.

I hadn't exactly been a monk in the 65 years after I'd lost her the first time, but I'd never again encountered anyone even remotely like her. The touch of her skin, the warmth of her body (no, vampires are not cold to the touch; if anything, we run a little hot), her firm softness, her soft firmness, the smell of her hair and her breath—somewhere along the line, I realized that my lovely Rumanian freedom fighter was the only girl with whom I'd ever been intimate who was not *dying*, however slow the process, or faraway the end. Each and every cell of her being was *alive*, in a way ordinary human beings are not.

There was time for intellectual curiosity. I was 80 years old, but I still got carded in bars. Surica was a year shy of 300 and although she took measures to avoid it—unlike every other woman in the world—still looked like the 17-year-old beauty she'd been when she was bitten.

And then there was Deabru, Richard Francis Xopher as he styled himself, a not-quite-human creature who had existed and preyed gorily on others, for as much as fifty millennia. Two huge questions about him:

First, I had tried drinking animal blood as an ethical substitute several times when I was new to this way of living. As a man, I could survive on it if I had to—the Maasai do it, and, to some extent, the Mongol warriors who conquered China, although it could be nasty—the virus was unimpressed, I got weaker and weaker until I fed it what it wanted.

So if Xopher really belonged to a different species—*Homo heidelbergensis*, Quyen had called it—how come he and his virus could be nourished by what to him must have seemed like animal blood? Did that mean I could live on the blood of a chimpanzee or a gorilla, both of which are extremely close, genetically speaking, to *Homo sapiens*?

Or how about a bonobo? I didn't know, and I didn't relish finding out. I'd get arrested at the zoo, and the media—unwilling to accept the simple truth that I was really truly a vampire—would accuse me of sexually molesting the apes. As I recall, there's a limerick about that.

"And what about genetic drift?" I demanded of Surica, who was discussing these matters with me while we waited—well, never mind what we were waiting for. "Every time that a cell replicates itself, there's a chance that a copying error will occur, producing something new. Odds are it will be lethal—we get cancer that way, and two-headed chickens—or destroyed by our immune systems, or not make any difference, but occasionally it's an improvement and that's how evolution happens. Wouldn't you think, after fifty thousand years, that Deabru would be a big lump of overlapping tumors or something by now?"

"Why do you ask me, my lovely man?" Surica answered, pouting a little, or pretending to: I was lying beside her in bed, naked, thinking about something other than making passionate love to her. "I was...well, let me see... 189 years old when I first heard of genetics."

"So you never wondered about this?" I asked.

"I didn't say that, darling. I became interested in genetics because of that very question. I never found an answer that satisfied me."

"How about this: viruses are communists—"

"They're what? Communists?"

"Sure. They bore their way into their host's cells, seize the means of production—or in this case, reproduction—and use it to turn out more viruses like themselves, instead of more cells like the host's."

"All right, I will give you that one. Very clever. Viruses are communists. I will also give you this—" She turned a little and laid something in my hand. The first part of her that I had ever touched.

About forty-five minutes later, she resumed our conversation. "So if viruses are communists, what does that tell us about genetic drift?"

She was as bad as I was, after all. "Only that this particular virus knows us intimately. It's large, as viruses go—I showed you—I'll bet it's large because it contains a copy of our blueprint, our DNA. With that information, it can take us back to when we were in prime condition—have you noticed how Anton looks younger every day?—and it can correct any errors in our replicated DNA that it may detect."

"Brilliant," she said. Is there some way to prove this?"

"I'm sure there must be, and once we're past this Deabru mess, I'll go right to work on it, probably with the help of Quinn and Quyen."

"Tell me, darling man, before you make love to me again. Aren't viruses always mutating? All those influenzas? What keeps ours from drifting?"

About an hour later, I told her I didn't have any idea.

31: DEEP AS THE MARROW

"He who does not punish evil, commands
it to be done."—Leonardo da Vinci

A week turned into two and then gave birth to three.

It wasn't so much that everyday life returns to its normal rhythms as that it imposes those rhythms whether we want it to or not. Mail, of the e- or snail variety, needs to get read and even occasionally answered. Garbage needs to be taken out to the alley. Clothes need to be washed and dried. Grass needs to be mowed, lest the city lawn Nazis have their way with us. Bills must be paid or they'll eventually turn off the water, the gas, the electricity, the TV cable, and all the fun.

We'd all been through the house thoroughly several times. I never bought the place with security in mind, for its defensibility, but now that was an issue. There was the front door, opening onto a glassed-in front porch with entrances inside to both my office and the living room. There was a back door, also to a glassed-in porch, leading into the kitchen. There was a side door coming into the kitchen from the garage.

The house was far from new. It didn't have a coal cellar like a lot of the older places do in New Prospect, with its slanting door covering a chute. It did have a delivery door in the kitchen, about three feet high, where milk used to appear every morning, back during a happier and safer time in our civilization's history. There were half a dozen basement windows and a couple of big skylights in the roof.

That's right: special glass in the skylights.

I spent a couple of long days—nights, actually—putting new catches, nails, and screws where they'd do the most good. Fresh air is better, but my central air conditioning would have to do for the duration.

Anton took what days of sick leave he had left—until now, he'd almost never been sick—and then had himself assigned to the night shift. Priscilla worked for herself and made her own hours. Normally that means a self-employed individual works 100 hours a week instead of only 40, but just now she was busy looking after her husband as he recovered.

Waiting for the other shoe to drop doesn't suit my temperament, and Surica had used up all of her patience—half a century's worth—in that Rumanian dungeon. Every night, we prowled the city, trying to find Xopher before he could finish healing so we could finish him altogether. I thought I'd known the city of New Prospect pretty well until I began patrolling every street and alley, every pathway in the park.

"Excuse me, sir," requested a whiskerless young rent-a-cop whose "beat" was one of our tonier gated communities, about a hundred square blocks of luxury bedrooms for folks silly enough to commute into the Denver smog every day, like lemmings. My lovely partner and I were gambling that the unprecedented number of fancy homes for sale, being repossessed, or abandoned might be tempting to our quarry: luxurious digs surrounded by what might as well have been fast food and gourmet restaurants everywhere. It was past two in the morning. The rentie had pulled up and climbed out of his company-marked Chevy HHR as I leaned against a lamppost listening to the neighborhood breathing in its sleep.

"This is private property, sir. Do you have some reason for being here?"

The boy's khaki uniform and ballcap made him look like a filling station attendant circa 1955. The clutter hanging on his wide, black, basket-stamped belt included a brand new full-sized Glock .40 and a couple of spare magazines. On summer days, he and his colleagues wore cargo shorts and rode Segways. Silliest goddamn thing I have ever seen.

As we talked, the radio on his belt conversed with itself.

"I'm a private investigator, officer. Tonight I'm looking for a missing person." Surica was a block away, sitting in the PT Cruiser. From there, I knew she could easily hear what the security guy and I were saying. I gave him a look at my credentials—an empty palm—and briefly described Xopher, adding, "He's mentally ill, extremely dangerous."

His eyes widened. "Maybe I should call it in then."

I *pushed* gently. "No need for that, son. Just keep your eyes peeled."

He grinned. "I can do that. Good night and good luck, sir."

"Thanks. Have a good evening." He climbed back into his little truck and was gone. I was curious about the HHR, but liked my Cruiser better.

As we had made our "rounds" earlier, Surica and I had talked about the future. Over the last six and a half decades, I had never really hoped to do that with anyone. So I had to ask, at least once in our lives.

"Why me, Surica? I know why I love you—"

She breathed; I loved the sight and sound of it. "Because, lovely man, you are the kindest, gentlest, sweetest person I have ever known."

"Hell of a thing," I told her, "to be saying to a vampire."

"Hell of a vampire to be saying it to. For what it is worth, you are also the fiercest, my darling. And I have never known anyone, in my almost three hundred years, who loves life the way you do. Most people merely end up dragging themselves through their three score and ten, grateful when it's finally over. If we can, we must have many children so you can teach them to love life the way you have taught me."

"Best offer I've had all day." I didn't know what else to say. If Surica and I survived this fight with her old nemesis, we would be truly free to make what we might of our lives, our love, and our immortality, together. We would start by sharing our gift with Priscilla, if she was willing. And we had a friend who needed a new leg.

As I watched the HHR's taillights dwindle in the gated suburban distance, Surica somehow managed to slip up soundlessly behind me, let one long, smooth leg with its high-heeled ankle-strap shoe escape the slitted skirt she was wearing (she has odd ideas about combat gear), and leaned against the lamppost, wrapping that leg halfway around the post.

She parted her lips...

It was almost a whisper. Looking up at me suggestively from under her long eyelashes, she was singing a very old, very familiar tune, familiar, that is, to any who'd lived through the Second World War, in a low, growly, ninety-nine and forty-four one hundredths percent sexy voice:

> *Vor der Kaserne,*
> *Vor dem grossen Tor,*
> *Stand eine Laterne*
> *Und steht sie noch davor.*
> *So woll'n wir da uns wiederseh'n,*
> *Bei der Laterne woll'n wir steh'n,*
> *Wie einst, Lili Marleen.*

I finished with her, "Wie einst, Lili Marleen." The song was very simple, about a soldier meeting his girl every night under the street lamp in front of an army post gate. It had been absurdly popular throughout the Forties, with guys in uniform on both sides of the line. The version I knew and liked best was by Marlene Dietrich, but there were dozens of others. I hadn't heard or thought about it in decades.

I grinned. It's good to have someone who's lived through all the years and events you've lived through yourself. I hadn't realized how lonely it can be, outliving everyone you know. I shuddered to think how it must be for Surica, who was a couple of centuries older than I was.

We never found a trace of Xopher, not that night. I wondered what—or who—he'd been eating and why we weren't finding any drained bodies. He was being uncharacteristically discreet in his dining habits.

I didn't like it.

When we got back home, Surica went upstairs. I stopped for a moment in my office to get the shotgun from a cabinet and take it upstairs with me. I didn't notice the dark form in the far corner of the room until it spoke, "You didn't expect me back quite so soon, did you?"

Surica chose that moment to come in from the hall door to the kitchen.

The voice from the shadows was unmistakable, but the rest was a big question mark, even when he moved into the light. Xopher—Deabru—was dressed, from head to toe, in a sort of body stocking, made of some very tightly knit black material that fit every contour of his body. Even the face, head, and hands were covered, and if you were to describe the garment as some kind of bandage, you wouldn't be far wrong.

He was also wearing dark, round goggles—like welding glasses—over his eyes. God alone knew what they looked like by now; Surica had shot them to pieces. Here and there areas of the surface of the suit glistened, where his movements apparently reopened his wounds. Blood and serum seeped into the fabric covering them until they closed again. He smelled like a freshly-opened grave. The creature also wore a wide-brimmed fedora, a long, khaki-colored overcoat, and black shoes.

"I didn't know what to expect," I told him conversationally. I'd been beating my brains for days, trying to decide what to say when this moment finally came. It might not matter, but it also might give us the only advantage we had. I stood beside my desk, my ugly Remington shotgun leaning against it. I told him, "I started getting ready for you the hour after you ran away. I'm ready now. So are my friends."

"Ran away?" Somehow, although I was taller, the apparition seemed to loom over me. "You wouldn't give me what I wanted, Mr. Gifford, even though what little I asked of you was comparatively simple and easy."

"I tried to tell you," I protested. "I have no idea—"

"Enough, human! It doesn't matter any more. You and your friends felt justified attacking me. You injured and thwarted me. Now your little blood-bitch will die as slowly and painfully as I can contrive, while you are forced to watch, after which I will end you the same way."

Xopher took an unexpectedly deep step forward, seized Surica by the wrist, and swung an arm up and backward to deliver her a disabling blow.

Not like herself at all, she shrank back, cowering. I felt my fangs erupt again—he seemed to have that effect on me—as I leapt for the monster's throat with clawed hands. Weakened as he was, he was still too fast for me. I took the fist and forearm he'd meant for Surica, which knocked me across the room, where I bounced off one corner of the desk, slid along the hardwood floor, and fetched up against a big bookcase that teetered, spilled books, and fell over on me.

He swept Surica up and crushed her throat in his powerful grip.

Before he could hurt her, though, she hit him so hard beneath the ribs that her little fist sank into his body to the spine. Stunned, he grunted in agony and staggered backward. As he threw Surica from him, I grabbed up the Remington 12 gauge from the floor where it had fallen and shot him, neither hearing the blast nor feeling the recoil which can ordinarily bring tears to my eyes. The deadly cargo of fine silver chain impacted Xopher's body, wrapping itself around him, cutting into his dark knitted clothing, burning its way through his smoldering flesh.

I worked the slide. A second and third shot ripped him nearly in half. As he fell, his enraged screams and bellows rattled the windows, indescribable and thoroughly non-human. As for me, I didn't stop shooting until the gun was empty and Xopher was a pile of fine, gray ash.

Surica threw herself, sobbing, into my arms.

32: THE SHAPE OF THINGS TO COME

"I don't want to achieve immortality through my work. I want to achieve it through not dying."—Woody Allen

*N*obody slept much the rest of that night.

We never found out how Xopher had gotten into the house. Anton and Priscilla, Quinn and Quyen, had all been occupied with separate tasks that evening but were in the house again before we got there. Your friendly neighborhood Chief of Detectives had been going from motel to motel, checking registries. Anton was discovering that individuals were absolutely delighted to give him answers when he asked the right way, and that the mother of his children made a pretty damned good partner.

The Kowalskis had stayed in, soaring the thermals of cyberspace, looking for answers in their own way. Once the ruckus had begun in my office—poor Surica had come down to see if I was *ever* coming to bed; it's very flattering—they'd all piled up in the doors, waving guns around like a bad Republic western, including Priscilla with her derringer.

Then it was time to clean up the mess.

Contrary to popular belief, the adult human body is only about 70 percent water. Uncle Smedley's "ashes" that we bring home from the funeral home aren't ashes at all, but dried and pulverized bone—about four pounds' worth. First they burn you and then they grind you up.

In the words of the immortal Durante, "It's humiliatin'." When our top sergeant in basic training had growled, "You guys wanna live forever?" I'd always answered "Hell, yes I do!", at least under my breath.

There was nothing like ground bone to Xopher, otherwise known as Deabru. Raising the room's temperature by at least 20 degrees in the process, he'd turned into something resembling what you'll find in the bottom of your barbecue grill at the end of the summer, and the hardwood floor in my office would never quite be the same. I vacuumed every bit of it up—there was an awful lot of it—and took the bag to the county landfill myself, where I risked arrest by being there at night and scattering the fine gray powder to the eternal Front Range wind.

Surica came with me, but she didn't offer to help. She watched me do it without expression on her face, but I had an idea what she was feeling.

Free.